LOST IN CANCUN

THE ROYAL RESORT SERIES

ROSE MARIE MEUWISSEN

Lost in Cancun
Digital/Print Edition
Copyright 2025 by Rose Marie Meuwissen
https://www.rosemariemeuwissen.com

Print ISBN: 978-1-954030-14-5
Published in the United States of America
Nordic Publishing
Edited by Leanore Elliot and
Rose Marie Meuwissen
Cover Design by Rose Marie Meuwissen

❀ Created with Vellum

To my Cancun friends Sue, Patti, Chrissy, Tom, Vicki and Reed, who have made our trips memorable and always managed to provide some sort of excitement. Dennis and I have enjoyed winter getaways at The Royal Islander for the past thirty years and look forward to many more at The Royal Haciendas. We love The Royal Resorts!

LOST IN CANCUN BLURB

It's the summer of 1994, and Anna Marie's life as a devoted single mother is about to explode around her ears.

A vacation to Cancun becomes a trip to her past when her high school sweetheart shows up at the same resort. She's never forgotten her first love but always believed he died in Vietnam. Anna Marie now wonders if he ever did love her? Why did he disappear and never bother to try to contact her? Can she trust him with the most precious part of her heart—her daughter?

Unsure about his future before leaving for basic training, James initiated a break-up only to realize that she expected a proposal. Their last encounter ended with Anna Marie in tears, and he was left drowning in guilt. So many times, he'd wanted to go back to Minnesota to beg for her forgiveness, but although brave in battle, he'd often blamed himself for taking the coward's way out and letting the years pass. Never in his wildest dreams did James expect to run into Anna Marie again.

Do they have a second chance at love?

LOST IN CANCUN

by

Rose Marie Meuwissen

PROLOGUE

It was their big day. The day they'd looked forward to their whole lives. Graduation Day! The culmination of their three years of high school and the end of life as they knew it. The graduation ceremony began in three hours.

James was picking her up in ten minutes. Anna Marie slipped her floral print cranberry-red sundress over her head, added the finishing touches on her makeup, puffed her hair up a little bit more, then added even more hairspray to be sure it stayed in place. After the graduation ceremony, the all-night party started, and they had all night to hang out with their friends and classmates.

James was her first boyfriend, they'd dated all through high school and even talked about getting married someday. Well, she had brought it up once. He'd explained that they were young and still had plenty of time to get married. But they were most definitely in love. She was sure of it. So why wouldn't they want to get married?

Of course, they each wanted to attend college first, but after graduating from college, they could get married. They hadn't actually talked about getting engaged, but more than a couple of her girlfriends had received engagement rings already. Mostly, on Prom night. She'd hoped to get one herself, but James hadn't proposed on Prom night. She kept her disappointment to herself and hadn't said anything to him. Weirdly though, he'd been rather secretive lately. She hoped and prayed tonight would be her big night and come tomorrow, she'd be wearing a beautiful diamond ring on her left hand.

The graduation ceremony took forever. At least, it seemed that way. It was held at the Metropolitan Sports Center. It was the only place large enough to hold the large graduating class and the enormous number of people who would be in attendance. There were 800 students in their Senior class, along with all their parents, siblings, relatives and friends who were there to watch them walk across the stage.

Sitting on her chair, where they were seated in alphabetical order, she couldn't help thinking that no matter what everyone said to the contrary, most of them would never see each other again. It was a big world out there and each one of them had their own destinies to pursue. At least, she knew James and her destinies would be on the same course.

The ceremony became boring and her mind wandered while she waited for her row to be ushered up to the stage area. Finally, her row was next. They stood in line, moving forward one person at a time. She now waited at the steps to the stage. Then she heard her name announced. *Anna Marie Johnson.* She climbed the steps up to the stage, accepted her diploma, shook hands with the principal, and walked to the opposite end of the stage to descend to the main floor. Luckily, the person in front of her knew where they were going because she felt as if she was in a daze.

At last, she watched James walk up to receive his diploma. His last name was Olson, so he was a few rows behind her. The very last name from their class was called three hours after the first one. By that time, everyone was dying to get out of the building.

Mass chaos erupted as students yelled and screamed, with graduation hats flying wildly into the air. James became lost in the crowd, and she could no longer see him. Her dad and mom came up behind her to offer hugs and congratulations. She found her best friend, Trudy Sandberg. They hugged, squeezing each other so tight they almost couldn't breathe. Presently, she found herself wrapped in strong male arms. She turned around and leaned up to kiss James.

"We did it!" she yelled. "We're done."

"Yes. We have our futures, our whole lives ahead of us." James looked into her eyes, staring into them, totally mesmerized. He placed his hands gently on her cheeks and kissed her.

She kissed him back, but the kiss felt different than usual. She couldn't quite put her finger on what it was, though. They had a party to get to, so she shrugged it off to the overexcitement of the day.

Anna Marie walked into the All-Night Party holding hands with James. This could be her big night! The group of friends they hung around with was beckoning them to join them. It was a bittersweet, long night filled with laughter, mixed with tears, as they shared stories about the last three years of high school. They played poker, various other games, watched videos, listened to bands and danced the night away.

At six in the morning, they walked to James' car to go home and get some badly needed sleep. He dropped her off at her parents' house and minutes later, she crawled into bed. Her mind was winding down from all the excitement of the day and night. The last thought before she fell asleep was that James had not proposed.

The next few weeks flew by. Their group of friends met at Lake Nokomis to go swimming, at the bowling alley to hold their own bowling tournaments, or at someone's house to play games or watch movies. Her friend, Trudy, was registered for Normandale Junior College, where Anna Marie would be attending. James had offers from the University of Minnesota, St. Cloud State and the University of MN Duluth. Anna Marie couldn't understand why he couldn't make a decision and simply pick one, but he kept insisting that choosing a college was a major decision and that he wanted to be sure he made the right choice.

In early August, Anna Marie put on her new floral-print, black, Gunnie Sax sundress and finished putting on her makeup. One by one, she took out the heated rollers from her hair, so her long blonde hair fell in curls over her bare shoulders. James would be picking her up shortly to go to dinner at Jax Café downtown. In her heart, she knew this would be the night he'd propose. She could hardly wait.

On the way home, James suggested they go to his house because his parents had gone to their lake cabin up on Mille Lacs Lake. They would ultimately be alone. This rare opportunity hadn't presented itself before. Anna Marie was still a virgin. She was deeply in love with James. Naturally, they had made out, went to second base and even third, but not all the way. The fear of getting pregnant in high school was too great, so they hadn't done *it*. Her friends were on the pill, but she just didn't trust it and she was deathly afraid of getting a blood clot, which could be a side effect.

They were done with school now, though. So, if she got pregnant, they could get married, which was what they'd planned anyway. All she needed was the ring.

At James' house, he turned on the stereo, lit candles, dimmed the lights, then poured two glasses of Boone's Farm Strawberry Hill wine.

An hour later, Anna Marie and James now felt the influence of the wine. They stood up and began slow-dancing to *Slow Hand* by the Pointer Sisters. James' hands roamed freely over her body as they swayed to the music in the flickering candlelight.

He kissed her and whispered in her ear, "I love you".

"I love you, too," Anna Marie replied.

The zipper on the back of her dress was slowly eased downward. Then it slid to the floor. His shirt was next. Minutes later, they were in his bedroom, lying naked in each other's arms. James quickly pulled out a condom and put it on. They both climaxed quickly and lay in each other's arms, relishing their first time.

James went to the bathroom to remove the condom. As he pulled it off, he realized it was leaking. There was a hole in it where it had ripped a little. He dropped it in the waste basket, making a note to take out the trash before his parents got back home. He didn't give the ripped condom another thought. Nobody got pregnant from having sex just once anyway. Right?

Anna Marie quickly dressed. James drove her home just in time to make her midnight curfew.

The next morning, James picked Anna Marie up and they went to Perkins for breakfast. Later, they met up with their friends to spend the afternoon at Lake Nokomis. That evening, after pulling up in her driveway, they walked up to the front steps and sat down.

"I wanted to let you know I've made my college decision," he said.

"Okay, what did you decide?" Anna Marie asked.

"I've decided to join the Army and I leave for basic training in the morning." James braced himself for her response.

"Are you serious?" she asked in shock.

"Yes. I have always wanted to fly airplanes and this is my best opportunity to do that." James fidgeted with his hands and glanced downward.

"How long will you be gone?" Anna Marie asked.

"I enlisted for four years." He now looked up at her.

"What does that mean for us?" She couldn't even believe they were having this conversation.

"I love you, but we're young and we need to see what else is out there before we make any lifelong decisions."

"You *are* breaking up with me, aren't you?" She gritted out the words, trying not to scream at him.

"Yes. You will be attending college, where you'll meet other guys. I want you to feel free to date them." James stood and began pacing on the sidewalk in front of the steps where she was still sitting. "I'm not sure I'll be coming back to Minnesota. Or at all. A lot of guys don't make it back."

"But...I thought..." Anna Marie couldn't stop the tears from rolling down her cheeks. Her world was crashing down in front of her. Instead of proposing marriage, he was breaking up with her!

"Anna Marie, I'm sorry. But this is for the best. Don't you understand? I want to see the world. Experience all it has to offer. I love you, but I can't promise I'll be back. Someday you'll thank me for setting you free." He kissed her as she clung to him. Gently, he moved away from her. He walked back to his car, got in and then drove away.

Anna Marie wiped the tears from her face, walked into the house and went directly to her room as quietly as possible. Thank God everyone was asleep. She tried not to cry anymore, but ended up crying herself to sleep.

The next morning, she waited for a phone call that never came. He'd left, not even bothering to call. She was no longer important to him. Her life was over. She'd lost her virginity and she'd lost her high school sweetheart all in the same night. Anna Marie was unsure what the future held. All she could hope for now was to meet someone new at college. And if not there, sometime in the future. But it hurt too much right now to think about being with someone else.

James was the love of her life.

A few weeks later, her love for James had turned into anger and she hated him for what he'd done. She had nothing to lose at this point, so she wrote him a letter. Instead of being filled with a profession of love, it was filled with a raging anger towards him. The letter acknowledged her deep hurt by what he'd done and how he'd left her standing on the doorstep without even asking her opinion on the situation. At the letter's end, she told him she hated him and never wanted to see him again. Ever! She mailed it to his parents' house, where she assumed they would forward it to him. She was over and done with James. Now she could forget about him and move on with her life.

CHAPTER 1

22 YEARS LATER, 1994
Minnesota

Anna Marie couldn't believe her daughter, Annika, would be graduating from Concordia College in May. Where had the years gone? Why was she still single? Those were the questions she kept asking herself. Her whole life, she thought someday she'd be married, but after James left, she'd never met anyone she felt she could trust again. And then having a daughter made it even more challenging to find a guy she would want as a father figure for her daughter. Unfortunately, no one had lived up to those expectations. Of course, she'd dated. And had sex. Eventually, she went on the pill after Annika was only two years old, because she'd finally felt ready to try dating but wasn't taking any chances on getting pregnant again.

Since it had always just been Anna Marie and her daughter, they were extremely close. Annika would be moving on to the next stage of her life after graduating, maybe even moving away. She had sent out resumes and was waiting to hear back from them. There was a huge possibility Annika would be leaving. It was time for Anna Marie to start her life over, perhaps even a chance to take up some hobbies.

Annika's best friend was Callie. They'd attended high school together, then went on to attend the same college. Fortunately, Anna Marie developed a best friend out of the deal, too. Callie's mother, Yvonne, became Anna Marie's best friend after attending their daughters' high school and college activities together for years. They were single moms, which brought them even closer on life's journey to raise their daughters alone.

Anna Marie and Yvonne were planning a vacation trip for themselves and their daughters to spend a week in Cancun after graduation. Anna Marie travelled all over the world for her job as a flight attendant for a small charter airline, Champion Air. She'd heard about a timeshare resort chain, The Royal Resorts, that consisted of five locations in the Cancun area. Sally Jenson, a fellow flight attendant, told her about The Royal Islander location and how she'd gotten a great deal in a villa for the weekend.

"Why don't you join me? It's more fun to spend the weekend with someone," Sally offered.

"Let me see if I can switch shifts. I'd really like to see the place for myself before booking it for Spring Break," Anna Marie said.

Anna Marie made a couple of calls and was able to switch shifts so she could spend the weekend in Cancun with Sally.

When they arrived at the resort, she wondered why she'd never spent any time in Cancun before. The resort was absolutely breathtaking. The beach consisted of white sandy beaches with the water an undeniably gorgeous turquoise color. The villas were like an apartment, including a large master bedroom, kitchen, dining area and living room. It had a large patio off the living room and bedroom. Oh, and of course...full view of the ocean. The villas could also include an attached lock-off unit with another bedroom, bathroom and mini-kitchen. It would be perfect for the vacation trip after graduation with Annika, Callie and Yvonne.

Mexico hadn't really been her cup of tea, but this resort was thoroughly Americanized, with the amenities being up to American standards. Which was one of the reasons she'd hardly spent any time in Mexico, believing it was a little too much on the primitive side for her tastes.

"I love it," Anna Marie said as they stepped out onto the patio deck. "This is so beautiful."

"I told you you'd like it!" Sally said excitedly.

"Let's put our bikinis on and go down to the pool." Anna Marie suggested as she quickly unpacked and changed into hers, then slipped on a beach cover-up. Thankfully, she'd been blessed with a great metabolism and still had a bikini body.

They walked down to the pool, oblivious to the men watching them walk through the lobby on their way out. After signing out their towels at the recreation building, they found two empty chairs by the quiet pool and lay down. The sun felt unbelievably good and warm after leaving Minneapolis, where it was currently -10 degrees. The temperature in Cancun was eighty and they were loving it. As flight attendants, they were always dealing with a case of jet lag, so once they allowed their bodies to relax, they both fell asleep.

James Olson, one of the CEOs at The Royal Resorts, was in the lobby of The Royal Islander when Anna Marie Johnson walked through on her way to the pool. He stopped dead in his tracks and had to steady himself.

"You okay, Sir?" the desk clerk asked James.

"I'm fine." James moved hesitantly toward the sliding glass door she'd just walked through.

Lately, he'd been re-evaluating his life decisions. Well, going over them in his mind anyway, and questioning if he'd made the right choices. Unfortunately, they always seemed right at the time. And most of them you couldn't go back and change, so what was the point of dwelling on them?

He'd never forgotten Anna Marie, after all, she'd been his first love. Ultimately, she'd ended up being the only real love of his life, which was why he'd never married. He'd done well for himself and there'd been many women through the years who would've married him if only he'd asked. Once you felt the fire and the magic of real love, it was way too hard to settle for less.

Which begs the question of why he hadn't tried to reconnect with Anna Marie? By the time he'd figured out she actually had been the one, he assumed it was way too late. After serving his four years in the Army, he spent the rest of his twenties and thirties flying for commercial airlines and moving from place to place, eventually ending up in Cancun. By then, he assumed she'd already found someone else and was undoubtedly married.

He couldn't believe she'd just walked into his resort! She hadn't changed at all, except she was older, of course, but still absolutely gorgeous.

James walked back into the lobby and up to the desk clerk. "Is there a guest by the name of Anna Marie Johnson registered?"

"I'll check, Sir." The clerk immediately began checking on the computer. "Yes, we do. Room 4223."

"How long is she staying?" he asked.

"Just for the weekend. They're checking out on Sunday."

"Who is in the room with her?" he asked.

"Sally Jensen. They're flight attendants for Champion Air."

"Thank you, Jose. That's all." James walked away and down the hall to the sales office, where a large wall of windows overlooked the pool area. He spotted her lying in a chair by the pool. Man, she was hot, even hotter than high school. He totally wanted to walk out there and talk to her, but it had been a significantly long time. Unfortunately, she undoubtedly still hated him for leaving that day.

He walked over to the sales office's reception desk. "Please send a bouquet of roses to room 4223."

"Do you want a note sent along with it, Mr. Olson?" she asked.

"Yes." He reached over the counter to write out what he wanted on the card and handed it to her. He wasn't sure it was even a good idea to send the flowers, but he still had to do it. "I want you to give her a certificate for a free week to come back and stay in the full villa and include the All-inclusive option."

"What reason should we give?" she asked.

"Say it was a promo from the sales department to specially selected guests," he said. "No one will turn down a gift."

"Just her? Not Sally, who she's staying with?"

"You're right. Yes, give one to both of them."

"I want to be notified when she books that week," he said and walked out.

Anna Marie had fallen asleep with the warm ocean breeze blowing gently over her body. Almost as if a feather had been gently brushing against her skin. The pool looked exceptionally inviting. All of a sudden, she had a strange feeling someone was watching her. Unfortunately, she had no idea where it came from at all. She stood to take a dip in the pool. For some reason, she couldn't shake the feeling someone was looking at her. She turned toward the main lobby building, where another room was connected to it with a wall of glass windows. Her eyes were drawn to a window where a man was looking out towards the pool. He looked away quickly so she couldn't see his face. He was conceivably an employee checking out the activity at the pool.

"Sally, I had a feeling someone was watching us. Did you notice anyone staring our direction?" Anna Marie asked.

"No. Maybe we have some guys checking us out?" Sally suggested.

"Maybe." Anna Marie shrugged as she moved towards the pool and descended the wide stairway leading to the inviting cool water.

Later that day, they saw a blinking light on the phone in their room. The message instructed them to check in at the front desk when they had a chance.

"What do you think that's all about?" Anna Marie asked.

"Haven't a clue," Sally answered.

"We can stop by the front desk when we go to dinner and check on it," Anna Marie suggested.

After changing into form-fitting little dresses and heels, they went downstairs to the lobby.

At the counter, Sally asked, "Can you check to see if you have any messages for us?"

"Certainly, madam," the clerk stated. He typed her info into the system. "It appears Pedro needs to talk to you. Just a moment, I'll have him come to the lobby."

Shortly, Pedro appeared at the front desk. "Ladies, please follow me. This way."

He led them into a large room that just happened to have a wall of glass windows overlooking the pool area. The same one where she'd seen the man looking out at her.

He motioned to a table where they sat down. "I have some good news for you young ladies," he said. "I see that you're only here for the weekend. The Royal Resorts would like to give each of you a certificate for a complete villa, good for one week to come back and stay with us again. There are no blackout dates and it's good for a year. As an added bonus, we are including the All-Inclusive for you and your guests."

"I don't know what to say," Sally said. "What is the catch? How much do we have to pay?"

"Nothing. It is completely free."

"But why are you giving this to us?" Anna Marie asked.

"It's our 30th anniversary this year and we're giving out these certificates randomly to guests staying with us. I guess it's simply your lucky day today." He handed each of them a folder with all the details and the certificate. "It appears you are on your way out to dinner. I won't keep you any longer." Pedro stood, so they stood and made their way to the door.

"Thank you," Anna Marie said, shaking his hand.

"Thank you, this is a most generous gift," Sally said, shaking his hand and then exiting the room.

After they reached the lobby, they stopped by the concierge to request a cab and walked outside to wait. It was still 75 degrees out with a beautiful, clear sky overhead. They had a clear view of the parking lot, where her attention was drawn to a new-style Corvette, where a man was getting into the driver's seat. A tall man who looked similar to the man she'd seen in the window.

What was going on with her? Why was she so obsessed with a man she hadn't literally seen clearly enough to even recognize again? She hadn't a clue.

Dinner at Harry's was delicious and the drinks were refreshing. All in all, it was a damn good day, which was all she had to say. It didn't stop there either, because when they got back to The Royal Islander and walked into their room, they were greeted by a dozen long-stemmed roses in a vase.

She looked over at Sally and they both threw up their hands. "Who do you think sent these?" Anna Marie asked.

"Haven't a clue. Maybe the elusive guy you thought was watching you?" Sally suggested.

"There's a card," Anna Marie said, picking up and opening the little envelope.

"So, what does it say?" Sally asked.

"Hope you enjoy your stay at The Royal Islander," Anna Marie read. "And it's signed—The Royal Resorts CEO, J. O."

"Well, not sure what to make out of everything that happened today. But who are we to complain about a free stay and beautiful flowers?" Sally walked over to smell the roses.

"I'm not complaining. The week's stay with All-Inclusive is worth about $3,500. I just hope I don't have some strange man watching me who turns out to be a stalker or worse."

"Awe, don't worry about it. Everything's fine."

The next morning, on their way to breakfast, they walked through the lobby toward the outside patio restaurant. It was filled with people from many different countries vacationing in the paradise of Cancun, Mexico. As they passed by the office for the timeshare sales department, Anna Marie stopped dead in her tracks and turned around in time to see the elevator door close only seconds after a tall, well-dressed man entered it along with two other men. They were having a conversation with their deep, husky, masculine voices. Which shouldn't be a problem, but for Anna Marie, it was.

The voice reminded her of a similar haunting voice from her past. A voice she hadn't heard for over twenty years. She stared at the man's back while the elevator door closed. What was wrong with her? She was certainly losing it. *There is no way it could've been him. Right?* And even if it was, she certainly didn't want to see or talk to him.

"Everything okay, Anna Marie?" Sally asked.

"Yes, sorry." She kept walking and tried everything she could think of to put James Olson out of her mind. She'd stopped thinking about him years ago. Why was he on her mind all of a sudden? She hadn't a clue, but this nonsense had to stop immediately. He hadn't shown up in over 20 years, and it wasn't ever going to happen in her lifetime.

Thankfully, she and Sally were heading back to the States in the morning. So, it would be the end of her feeling like James Olson could come walking around a corner at any time.

CHAPTER 2

Money had always been tight for Anna Marie as a single parent. She'd been lucky to have a good job with the airlines, complete with an excellent benefits package, but sending her daughter to college was her primary goal. Helping pay for college was something she'd wanted to do, to the point of her picking up extra shifts whenever possible to help as much as she could. Of course, Annika would still have student loans to pay, and Anna Marie intended to keep helping as much as she could.

The gift of a week-long stay in Cancun, complete with the All-Inclusive package, was so totally unexpected and overwhelmingly gracious on the resort's part. She felt so appreciative and unbelievably thankful. This package, along with her flight benefits, would enable her to give her daughter a fantastic graduation gift. It would also allow her to invite her best friend, Yvonne, and her daughter, Callie, to join them as well. Graduation was at the end of May, and their trip was planned for the first week in June. She wanted to plan it right afterwards, so if Annika was offered a job soon, they would still be able to take the trip.

Once Annika landed a job, she wouldn't be able to get away for presumably six months to a year, and there was a strong chance she would be moving out of state. Tears filled Anna Marie's eyes. The thought of Annika leaving actually terrified her. After college graduation, the graduate's life would never be the same.

She'd heard this often in the last few years. Sadly, no one ever mentioned how it would affect a single mom. She'd spent her whole life after her own graduation taking care of and raising her daughter. Annika had become her entire life. Soon Anna Marie's life would be changing, and for the first time, she would be on her own. Alone. She'd never been alone, and it was somewhat terrifying.

"Do I look okay, Mom?" Annika asked while she stared into the full-length mirror.

"Absolutely beautiful," Anna Marie said. "Ready to go?"

"I'm so excited. I did it!"

"Yes, you did, Baby. I'm so proud of you." Anna Marie hugged Annika and lightly kissed her on the forehead. "I love you."

"I love you, too, Mom." Annika hugged her mom back.

Anna Marie felt her eyes begin to tear up. "We need to go before I start crying." She released Annika as they walked out of Annika's bedroom.

At Concordia University's Luther Hall, where the graduation ceremony was held, Anna Marie and Yvonne sat in the parents' section waiting for their daughters to cross the stage and receive their diplomas. Annika received a degree in Marketing and Callie's was in Graphic Design. Thankfully, Yvonne had thought to bring a box of tissues along, as they both found themselves crying tears of happiness as their daughters received college diplomas. Their baby girls were now college graduates!

The following Saturday morning, the four headed to the airport in Anna Marie's SUV. One of the perks of working for Champion Air was that employees received a parking pass to park free in the airport ramp, even if it happened to be for a whole week of vacation days. Working for Champion also had the perk of 10 free confirmed passes each year, so they wouldn't have to fly standby.

They arrived at the resort around one to clear skies, bright sunshine and 85 degrees. The girls were excited to change into their bikinis and go to the beach. Anna Marie waited in the check-in line while the girls checked out the pool area. Finally, it was her turn. After filling out the paperwork, she was handed the keys to a beach-front villa on the 4th floor. The bellman loaded their bags onto a cart, and they followed him to their villa. They walked in, immediately drawn to the balcony, where they all stood in awe, watching the turquoise ocean waves rolling into the shore below them. The expansive white sand beach beckoned to them. Anna Marie walked back inside to give the bellman a tip as he set the last bag down in the room.

Annika and Callie quickly grabbed their bags to unpack so they could change. "See you at the beach," the girls yelled as they headed out the door.

"Okay. Save us chairs," Anna Marie called after them.

Anna Marie and Yvonne just smiled at each other as they took their bags into their rooms to unpack. Afterwards, they too put on their swimsuits and headed to the beach.

"This resort is beautiful," Yvonne commented. "Thanks for inviting us."

"Wouldn't have wanted to spend this week with anyone else but you and Callie."

They slipped on their swimsuit cover-ups and headed to the beach. Assuming the girls hadn't picked up towels, they stopped at the sports desk window to get towels for all of them. Spotting the girls on the beach, they descended the steps to the white sand and joined them. Soon, all four were relaxing on their towel-covered chairs in the warm sunshine.

CHAPTER 3

JAMES CHECKED THE GUEST RESERVATIONS EVERY DAY FOR ANNA Marie's name. When he eventually saw her name on the list for the first week in June, he felt excitement and anticipation like he'd never felt before. While at the same time, he was scared to death. This would most likely be his one and only chance to talk to Anna Marie again. Well, actually, he undoubtedly needed to apologize first. Then, if she was still listening to him, hadn't slapped his face and walked off, he might stand a chance of having a conversation with her.

He'd thought about trying to find out what she'd been doing all these years, but decided he would rather ask her in person. What he wasn't sure about was how he would approach her. The week before her arrival, he was a stressed-out mess. What was wrong with him? He regretted how he'd left her. But the real question was, why did he care so much about what her reaction would be? They hadn't seen each other since the summer after high school graduation, but they'd been high-school sweethearts, and that would undoubtedly make their meeting awkward.

At last, today was the day, and he still hadn't figured out how he was going to introduce himself to her. He sat in the back office of the front desk. It had a window, allowing him to see what was going on at the front desk, but it didn't allow the people to see into the back office. Finally, there she stood looking beautiful even after traveling for half the day. He'd made sure she had received a penthouse villa— one of the best ones at the resort. Apparently, she'd brought two young girls and a friend with her. He did feel curious about the young girls who soon left, presumably headed to the beach.

As soon as Anna Marie and her friend left, he walked out to the front desk. He asked for her sign-in sheet, and the clerk handed it to him. He wasn't sure what he hoped to find on it, but when he saw the names — Anna Marie Johnson, Annika Johnson, Yvonne Sandberg, and Callie Sandberg — it became apparent it was most likely two mothers and their daughters. *Anna Marie had a daughter.* It wasn't what he was expecting, but then he wasn't sure what he expected. A lot of things could've happened in twenty-plus years. Now he just had to figure out the best way to introduce himself to her after all this time.

Well, he didn't have a clue how he intended to do this, so he was going home before he did or said something stupid. James walked out to the parking lot to his two-year-old red Corvette convertible. Five minutes later, he pulled into his driveway and inside his extra-deep double garage. He'd built his home on the beach after he'd made his first million dollars.

When he arrived in Cancun after serving in the war with his Army buddies, they'd seen the white sandy beaches and turquoise, yet clear water. It was definitely a place where they wanted to spend more time. The land was cheap, so they'd bought large sections of it for investment and some for personal use. Since they'd been pilots in the Army, they were able to land jobs with the commercial carriers. After working for 10 years with the airlines, they were able to pay off the land loans and save enough money to build a timeshare resort where people could purchase a week of vacation in paradise on a 30-year lease.

The villas were similar to a small apartment, including a living room area, two bedrooms, two bathrooms and a full kitchen. Complete with a balcony overlooking the ocean. The owners wanted others to be able to enjoy the beautiful white-sand beaches and tropical climate. But ultimately their final goal was to make money, so they could live in Cancun on a full-time basis. Not permanently, but almost. They, of course, would still keep their US citizenship and maintain a home in the States, too.

James built a 7,000 square foot house on the Cancun beach only five years after their first resort opened. That had been a long time ago, and he'd just finished an update remodel on the whole house last year. It looked brand-new, featuring every modern convenience you could ask for. The house was a two-story white modern Mexican-style home with a large deck facing the ocean, located just a five-minute walk down the beach from The Royal Islander.

Thomas Sandberg, his friend from the Army and business partner, owned the property and house next door. They could see each other from their decks. At this moment, he could see Thomas standing on his deck talking with his son, Michael, and a couple of his friends. He knew the boys liked to hang out on the deck to look for girls. Heck, they were young, only in their early twenties, and that's what boys did. Not that he could fault them for it, back in the day when he was much younger, he used to do the same thing. He was much too old for that these days. It seemed like he kept getting older, and the women walking the beach kept getting younger.

There was no denying that Anna Marie's daughter, Annika, was an extremely attractive young woman. Heck, she was the spitting image of Anna Marie when she was young. Which made him wonder who her father was. Was it someone he knew? Was he still around? Was Anna Marie married to him at one time? He made a point of checking whether she was wearing a wedding ring when she was at the check-in counter, but her ring finger was bare.

Out of the corner of his eye, he saw the boys, Michael and Samuel, leaving the deck at a rapid speed. They were eagerly heading to the beach to make contact with some young women they'd seen walking the beach who'd caught their interest. As he watched intently to see who their latest conquests would be, his mouth dropped open. Sure enough, it was Annika and Callie, just strolling along the beach leisurely, without a care in the world.

He wouldn't personally break up these young people's fun for the afternoon. But that was as far as it would go. Annika was with Anna Marie, and he needed to make sure nothing happened to her while she was in Cancun. He knew what was on the boys' minds, and it wasn't going to happen this time. Not when he could stop it. Michael was a great kid and almost like a son to him. But boys were boys, and those testosterone hormones went crazy in young men. He was definitely keeping an eye on this situation.

Minutes later, Michael was introducing himself to the girls. Soon, they were all laughing and smiling as the four continued walking down the beach. Michael was a level-headed young man. James could only hope he would make better choices with the women in his life than he had. And have no regrets.

James had spent all his time off from flying building The Royal Resorts business. Finding someone to spend his life with and start a family had sadly not been a priority. He regretted how he'd handled his breakup with Anna Marie, the one person he'd truly loved. With her, he'd seen the possibility of marriage and children, but he'd been young and clueless.

So many times, he'd wondered what would've happened if they hadn't broken up on the day he'd left for the Army. They'd had something special. At the time, he hadn't realized it, though. Regret filled his thoughts as the years passed by. He'd never found that connection with anyone else. If she gave him a second chance, he would not screw it up this time.

CHAPTER 4

"Mom, we met these incredibly hot guys from the States while we were walking on the beach," Annika said.

"That's nice. Just remember, nothing permanent will come from this chance meeting," Anna Marie said.

"Exactly. But have fun. Just not too much fun," Yvonne added.

"Mom, we know. But we can have a little fun," Callie said. "We've managed to make it through four years of college. I'm sure we can make it through one week in Cancun. And we do have our moms along in case you haven't forgotten."

They all laughed.

"You can tell us about them while we get ready to go to dinner. Are you thinking casual or fancy tonight?" Anna Marie asked.

"Heck, since it's all inclusive, we might as well go for fancy!" Annika suggested.

They all agreed. After they all took refreshing showers, put on sexy sundresses, makeup and jewelry, they headed across the street to Captain's Cove over on the side of the bay, which overlooked the lagoon. Their luck held out, and they got a table outside overlooking the water.

Anna Marie was accustomed to cutting corners to make ends meet, so it was an absolute extravagance to walk into a fancy restaurant and have the luxury of ordering whatever she desired off the menu. And being able to treat her daughter, Yvonne and Callie to the same opportunity was something she still wasn't sure how it had even happened. One thing she knew for sure, she was going to enjoy every minute of it.

After dinner, as they were leaving, Anna Marie glanced over at the other people in the dining area, and in the far corner, a man caught her eye. Their eyes met for a moment, but in that moment, she witnessed the familiar face from her past staring back at her with recognition. She looked away quickly and kept walking. The speed of her steps increased rapidly, which wasn't easy in heels, but she needed to get out of here as fast as possible.

Annika ran up behind her, where she'd stopped to cross the street because the light was red. "Mom, is something wrong?"

"I'm fine. Just needed some fresh air, that's all." Anna Marie kept her eyes focused on the street light.

"You practically ran out of there," Annika stated.

"I'm fine." Anna Marie desperately tried to slow her rapid breathing down. She wasn't fine, and obviously, she didn't look fine either. Quickly, she turned back towards the restaurant, looking for what she wasn't sure. There wasn't anyone at the entrance. Did she honestly expect to see James standing there? Was it him sitting at that table? It couldn't be. The fates could not be that cruel.

The light promptly turned green, but before she moved forward to cross the street, she looked back again, only this time towards the parking lot. She didn't know what she was looking for, but then she spotted it. The red Corvette convertible. Immediately, she turned back toward the street to follow the girls and Yvonne across to the other side of the road. Her head was filled with the memory of that red Corvette and the man getting into it the last time she was in Cancun. Plus, that weird feeling of déjà vu. Now she knew why. But what were the odds he'd be down here again at the same time she was? Probably like a million to one. *Get a grip, girl. Everything will be all right.*

The girls walked on ahead.

Yvonne walked up next to her. "You, okay?" she asked.

"Not really. I'll tell you about it later when the girls aren't around," Anna Marie said softly, managing to sound somewhat convincing.

"Sure. Later," Yvonne said.

When they arrived back at the resort, the girls walked through the lobby toward the outside bar. A breeze blew gently off the ocean under a star-filled sky. Such a lovely evening to sit outside and have a drink. Heck, the drinks were free. They all ordered—Mudslides and Banana Monkeys.

Annika and Callie sat down at a table, while Yvonne and Anna Marie waited at the bar for the drinks.

"Anna Marie, are you sure you're okay? You look exceptionally pale. Back at Captain's Cove, all the color drained from your face, and you looked like you'd seen a ghost." Yvonne kept her eyes focused on Anna Marie.

"I did," Anna Marie half mumbled. That pretty much summed up the situation. Yes, she had seen a ghost. A part of her had always thought maybe James had been killed in the war, but then again, she'd never heard that from anyone. But at least if he'd died, he would've had a certifiably good reason for not coming back home to her.

"Not sure you should have another drink right now," Yvonne stated as four drinks were set in front of them.

"I'm fine, trust me." Anna Marie picked up her drink and Annika's, then walked over to the table where the girls were sitting. She handed Annika the Banana Monkey, just as two incredibly nice-looking young men approached the table.

"Hola. We were just in the area and decided to see if you girls were at the bar," one of the guys said.

"Hi, Michael. Samuel," Annika said. "Would you care to join us?"

"Yes, please do," Callie added.

"Oh, this is my mom, Anna Marie, and Callie's mom, Yvonne."

Both boys came over to shake hands with Anna Marie and Yvonne. "Do you mind if we join your daughters?" Michael asked, flashing them a huge smile, revealing perfect white teeth.

"No, go right ahead. We'll take a different table and let you young people get to know each other." Yvonne walked over to a different table on the other side of the outside patio and sat down. Anna Marie followed and joined her.

"Okay, now tell me what is going on," Yvonne practically ordered once she sat down.

"You know how I told you Annika's father left after high school graduation to join the Army. We had sex the night before, and that's how I got pregnant. I never heard from him again and didn't know what happened to him, so I told Annika he died."

"Why are you bringing this up now?" Yvonne questioned.

"When you said I looked like I'd seen a ghost, you were right." Anna Marie stared out toward the setting sun sinking into the ocean.

"Oh my God. What on earth are you talking about?" Yvonne snapped her fingers to get her attention.

"I saw James at the Captain's Cove restaurant tonight." Anna Marie picked up her drink and took a sip.

Yvonne took a sip of her drink. "Well, you don't know that he's dead. It could be him."

"Exactly. That's my dilemma," Anna Marie stated, taking another sip of her delicious frozen Mudslide drink.

"Maybe we should walk back over to the restaurant and see if this man you think might be James is still there?" Yvonne asked.

"And do what? Do you think I'm going to talk to him? He left me pregnant and never came back. Granted, I told him in a letter that I never wanted to see him again," Anna Marie stated firmly. "Not happening."

"Yes, I think that's exactly what you should do."

"I don't ever want to speak to him again. That was a long time ago. Everyone has moved on, and there isn't anything I have to say to him." Anna Marie glanced over toward Annika's table.

"How about that he has a daughter?" Yvonne asked.

"Right, that would be a great ice-breaker, wouldn't it?" Anna Marie countered.

"Did he see you? Do you think he recognized you?" Yvonne fired off the questions.

Anna Marie sipped her drink. "He looked right at me, our eyes met. I don't know if he recognized me."

"No wonder you went running out," Yvonne concluded.

"You know, the odd thing is that the last time I was down here with Sally, I felt like someone was watching me. And then there was a man I only saw from the back, who got into a red Corvette. It was an eerily odd feeling I got, though, when I saw him. Almost a Déjà-vu thing. And I saw the red Corvette parked at Captain's Cove." Her hand started to shake, and she was sure her face had a red tint since her whole body felt flushed.

"Anna Marie, you have to go talk to him," Yvonne said.

"I've spent my whole life hating him. That's not going to change, so what's the point?" Anna Marie questioned.

Yvonne nervously shifted in her chair. "Maybe he had a good reason for not contacting you."

Anna Marie stared blankly into her drink. "Yeah, he didn't want to."

"Anna Marie..."

Anna Marie cut her off, "Listen, if he wants to talk to me, he's going to have to make the first move."

Annika walked over to their table. "Mom, we're going to go to the bar at the hotel next door called The Royal Caribbean. According to the guys, they have a DJ and dancing on Saturday nights. Okay?"

Anna Marie remembered from her previous stay that both hotels were owned by the same company, and you could easily walk between them. "Sure. Don't stay out too late. We'll see you back in the room. Do you have a key?" She'd successfully put her emotions on autopilot so Annika wouldn't notice her uneasiness and anxiety over James.

"Yes." Annika held up her key. "We won't be out past one." She left and walked back to the table where Callie and the guys waited for her.

Annika, Callie and the guys got up and walked towards The Royal Caribbean.

Anna Marie and Yvonne watched them leave as they leaned back in their chairs, staring out over the pool and ocean behind it.

Yvonne picked up her drink and held it in the air. "Here's to the empty nest time of our lives!"

Anna Marie picked up her drink and clinked it against Yvonne's glass. "To new beginnings! Hopefully, the ones we want and choose!" She subtly glanced back toward the lobby.

CHAPTER 5

JAMES COULD TELL SHE HAD RECOGNIZED HIM BY THE LOOK IN her eyes. He wasn't sure what he'd expected her reaction to be, but he hadn't thought she'd go running out of the restaurant. She'd almost looked like she'd seen a ghost. Had she believed he'd died in the war? That was definitely a possibility and would explain her reaction.

Their breakup over twenty years ago had haunted him many times throughout the years. He regretted how he'd left things and sincerely wanted a chance to apologize to her. He didn't deserve her forgiveness but desperately desired it.

He followed her to the door, but waited too long because when he got there, they'd already gone back to The Royal Islander. *Should he follow her back to the resort?* Hell, if he knew what he was doing! He was in the parking lot trying to decide, but couldn't, so he got in his Corvette. Then, instead of going home, he found himself pulling into The Royal Islander's parking lot. Hell, it was only a block, he could've easily walked. He parked and sat in the car, pondering the situation. Mentally going over his options.

Rushing her wasn't what he had in mind, but she would only be in Cancun for a week. This was day one, so only six days were left.

He got out of the car and walked into the lobby of The Royal Islander. As an owner, he always tried to keep a low profile and asked the staff not to address him in public while he was there. The last thing he wanted her to know was that he was one of the resort's owners. At least not until he was able to talk to her.

Standing in the doorway leading from the lobby to the pool and outside bar area, he could see Anna Marie and her friend seated at a table. Their daughters, along with Michael and Samuel, were walking towards The Royal Caribbean. *Probably heading to the bar to go dancing.* Annika was Anna Marie's daughter, and nothing was going to happen to her while she was in Cancun. Nothing at all on his watch. He needed to have a talk with the boys and let them know Annika and Callie were off-limits. Absolutely no messing around. No sex. Not with these two young ladies.

There Anna Marie was, as beautiful as ever and sitting only a mere fifty feet away from him. Well, it was now or never. He walked out the lobby's glass doors toward the bar.

"Okay," Yvonne said. "I don't know what James looked like back then, but there is a remarkably striking, tall man wearing an impeccable, clearly custom-made, navy suit walking towards the bar. You can't see him because he is directly behind you."

"Oh my God! Is it him?" Anna Marie asked in a somewhat hushed voice.

"Like I said, I don't have a clue what he looks like—maybe you should take a quick look to see if it's him?" Yvonne asked.

"I don't think I can." Anna Marie trembled nervously, feeling like she was eighteen again.

"Well, regardless of what you can or can't do, he's coming up right behind you," Yvonne stated.

"Damn." Anna Marie looked down at her hands, clasped tightly together.

"He's fortunately pretty cool for an older man. If you don't want him, I'll take him!" Yvonne continued watching his approach.

"Yvonne! How close is he?" She slowly raised her head to look up.

"Right here," Yvonne said as the man walked directly up to their table.

"Anna Marie Johnson." He looked into the eyes of the woman who'd won his heart so many years ago.

Anna Marie searched his face as she experienced complete nostalgia, all those happy memories and dreams of a life together with him that she'd locked away so many years ago. His features had matured, but he was still incredibly handsome. With a chiseled jawline, his face was deeply tanned. A face she thought she'd never see again. He was no longer the boy she knew in high school, and now seemed like a complete stranger. She couldn't speak.

"James Olson. We went to Richfield High School together. It's been a long time, not sure if you'd still recognize me. But I was certain it was you at the restaurant." He extended a hand to shake hers, but she didn't respond. His worldly demeanor spoke of complete confidence.

Slowly, she stood, and he moved closer, stopping only inches from her body. The shock she felt was overwhelming, and the urge to say nothing but walk away was immense. Her heart was beating so rapidly in her chest, she could hardly breathe. At last, she found her voice. "I assure you that the words I would like to say to you, you would not want to hear. Goodbye." Anna Marie could not walk away fast enough. She didn't look back but instead headed straight for the lobby and to the elevator that would take her to her room and away from him. James Olson. The man who'd broken her heart so many years ago.

Yvonne and James stared at her retreating body passing through the glass sliding doors into the lobby.

"I'm not sure what just happened here, but I think I need to go see if she's all right," Yvonne said and headed in the same direction Anna Marie had gone.

James didn't respond but instead sat down at the table and waved down a waiter to bring him a glass of whiskey. He chanced a glance at the lobby just in case she changed her mind and came back.

It was empty.

Maybe he'd used the wrong approach? He was in uncharted territory and had no idea how to talk to her. He was a businessman in Mexico, where he had taught himself to be the confident and strong man he was today. Apparently, hoping she would respond to this version was the wrong tactic. When she knew him in high school, he was still just a boy, vastly different from the man he was today, but in his heart, he was the same person who'd loved her all those years ago.

An hour passed, and he still sat at the table alone. He looked up towards the balcony of her penthouse villa and saw that the lights were on. At this point, he could only assume she wasn't coming back to talk to him.

CHAPTER 6

How could a relaxing week on the beach in a tropical location turn into a nightmare? She wasn't sure she'd slept at all, since all she remembered about last night was waking up multiple times because she kept seeing James' face in her dreams. Unless he was actually intent on stalking her, avoiding him shouldn't be all that hard.

"Mom, are you going to stay in bed all morning?" Annika asked. "We're ready to go down and have breakfast."

"Okay, I'm up. Let me take a quick shower first."

"Hurry up, then." Annika bent down, kissed her mom on the cheek, and left the room.

Thirty minutes later, they were on their way to the breakfast buffet, complete with made-to-order waffles and omelets. Anna Marie scanned the restaurant before sitting down at their table. Luckily, James wasn't among the guests already seated. She actually relaxed enough to enjoy her coconut-pecan waffle with coconut and Caramel syrup. It was delicious!

Why was she so worried about seeing James? It wasn't so much him, but most likely her fear of Annika's reaction to finding out he was her father. Oh, and the part about him not actually being dead. That would take some explaining from James. Mainly, she was afraid Annika would think she'd been lying to her all these years. But was it exactly lying when she honestly had no idea if he'd made it home from the war? She really didn't have an excuse except that she thought it was best for both of them to assume he was dead.

Today they were going to find chairs on the beach and go swimming in the ocean. At least that was the plan so far. They weren't at the beach very long before Callie spotted Michael and Samuel approaching. They pulled up chairs, and before long, the four headed to the shore to take a swim in the ocean. Anna Marie and Yvonne politely declined, opting to remain relaxing in their chairs on the beach and watch their belongings.

"Anna Marie, what are you going to do about James?" Yvonne asked after the four of them left.

"Not one damn thing. Hopefully, he got the hint and will not show up again."

"Maybe he's staying at the resort, too?" Yvonne offered.

"Hadn't thought of that! Ohhh...That could be bad." Anna Marie sat up and closed the book she'd been reading.

"Or good?"

"I don't want to talk to him." Anna Marie closed her eyes and lay back down on her lounge chair.

"I think you made that pretty clear." Yvonne turned over onto her stomach.

"Exactly."

Yvonne set her book on the table. "But I do think you should just talk to him, or you may regret it. Potentially for the rest of your life."

"Oh Hell! What am I going to do? If I talk to him and he figures out that Annika is his daughter...it could devastate her." Anna Marie sat up and set the book on the table beside her chair.

"He is her dad. Do you genuinely want to deprive her of meeting him? Might be for the best. He certainly has aged well. Maybe you and James are getting a second chance? And Annika?"

"Hell, no! He left, and even when he was done in the Army, he obviously could've come back to me. To Minnesota. But he chose not to. Keep that in mind. And I don't care how damned hot and sexy he looks, he doesn't deserve a second chance. Not after all these years."

"Well, good to know you're not dead yet." Yvonne chuckled, turned over, and sat up in her chair, scanning the beach for the girls.

"What?" Anna Marie asked her.

"At least you recognized he's one sexy man. And he wants to talk to you."

"I'm not talking to him. I don't have anything to say to him." Anna Marie knew that was a lie she'd been telling herself for way too many years. Unfortunately, it simply wasn't true.

Yvonne scanned Anna Marie's face. "Really? I think it sounds like you have a lot you'd like to say to him. Probably thought about it for over twenty years. Might be good for you to get it all out there while you have the chance."

Anna Marie and Yvonne ended their conversation abruptly. Annika, Callie, Michael and Samuel came running across the white sand beach back to their chairs.

"Mom, you should go in the ocean! It's so much fun!"

"Not today," Anna Marie replied. "I'm going to take a walk down the beach, though. Can you stay here and watch our stuff?"

"Sure, Mom." Annika sat down in her chair.

"I'll join you, Anna Marie." Yvonne got up and followed her to the shoreline.

"You didn't have to come along." Anna Marie kept walking.

"I know. Thought you could use the company, and besides, we need some exercise to keep our bodies in shape." Yvonne laughed.

Not too far down from The Royal Islander, they passed a few private residences mixed in between the high-rise hotels.

"How odd that these homes are still here." Anna Marie took in the beauty of these stately houses proudly overlooking the turquoise ocean.

"Must be awfully wealthy people who own them that they

haven't sold out to some large hotel chain by now," Yvonne commented.

"Exactly. Who has that kind of money?" Anna Marie questioned.

"Obviously, there are people who do." Yvonne continued walking.

After walking to the next hotel, The Omni Hotel, they turned around and made their way back, walking on the edge of the shore just close enough to get their feet wet when the rolling waves made their way up the shoreline.

"Glad you're back. We're starving!" Annika exclaimed happily. "Let's have lunch up at the poolside restaurant."

Annika and Callie began gathering up their things.

"We'll see you later." Michael waved as he and Samuel walked down to the shoreline and away from them.

Minutes later, they were seated at the pool café, enjoying lunch.

"Michael mentioned a place called Coco Bongo. It's the Mexican version of a Cirque du Soleil show. He said it was somewhere we should go to get a real Mexican show experience. Do you want to go tonight?" Annika asked.

"It sounded fun from what he was saying." Callie's face lit up with excitement.

"Any idea how much it costs?" Anna Marie couldn't help always worrying about the money.

"No. But I thought I read on your voucher for the room that two excursions/tours were included per person." Annika got up, walked over to the tour desk to pick up a brochure on the tours and came back to the table.

"Okay, we can check it out. What else did you girls want to do while we're down here?" Anna Marie asked.

"I heard Playa Del Carmen is fun. Lots of shops and restaurants. And you can take a ferry across the water to Cozumel, too," Callie offered.

"Not to change the subject, but are Michael and Samuel from the States?" Yvonne asked.

"Michael's dad has a place here in Cancun, but he's actually from Colorado." Annika's face lit up as she conveyed the answer. "He just graduated from the University of North Dakota's School of Aerospace Sciences in Grand Forks."

"Wow, good for him. Sounds like he knows what he wants to do with his life," Anna Marie commented.

"Samuel's dad has a house here in Cancun, too, but he's actually from Montana. He graduated from the University of North Dakota in Grand Forks with Michael," Callie offered.

Yvonne's relief was evident on her face. "They both sound like nice guys."

"Mom, were you expecting them to be a couple of beach bums or something?" Callie asked.

"More like, hoping they weren't." Yvonne smiled.

One by one, they all burst out laughing.

Anna Marie scanned the other tables at the café and the pool area. No James. So far, so good. Maybe her reaction had scared him off enough never to return! Unfortunately, she doubted that would be his response to her words. They had unfinished business. He knew it, and regrettably, deep down she knew it too.

CHAPTER 7

THE NEON LIGHTS OF COCO BONGO FLASHED IN SYNC, beckoning potential customers to approach the open doors. The pulsating music reverberated with the loud, club-style beats, which coursed through their bodies even before they entered the building. Anna Marie and Yvonne nodded their heads in a *'What have we gotten ourselves into?'* expression. But seeing the looks of excitement on their daughter's faces, they said nothing as they followed them into the Coco Bongo nightclub.

"This wasn't what I was expecting, but then again, I didn't have any idea what to expect." Anna Marie looked around at all the young people in skin-tight pants and bare stomachs.

"Gotta say this makes me feel old," Yvonne answered as they meandered their way through wall-to-wall people. The music was so loud it made having any type of conversation difficult.

Fortunately, they had VIP tickets with a reserved table, because the thought had crossed Anna Marie's mind to turn around and walk right back out. No matter how old the girls were, they were only college graduates and still had a lot to learn. She had protected Anna Marie as much as a mother could, and God only knew how hard it was to let go even when she was trying her hardest. As they took their seats at a high-top table, she didn't miss all the stares the girls attracted from the young men at the bar and nearby tables. She didn't trust one single guy in the bar as far as her daughter was concerned.

Anna Marie recalled the news reports she'd heard about drinks being laced with drugs in Mexico, and multiple people had actually died. Hell, she was afraid to order a drink at this place. *Am I being paranoid?* Maybe, but just to be safe, she wouldn't order a drink. The water bottle she had in her purse would be just fine. Yvonne opted for the water bottle in her purse, too. However, the girls walked over to the bar and ordered drinks.

"Kind of overwhelming. This scene is rather out of my comfort zone," Yvonne said.

"Me, too." Anna Marie had her eyes glued to the bar where the girls waited for their drinks. Two young men approached them, displaying interested grins. They appeared to be locals by their Mexican coloring and the comfortable ease with which they carried themselves. They were extremely good-looking, so it was apparent why the girls would be drawn into a conversation with them.

The lights dimmed even lower than they already were, and the show started. Acrobats dropped from the ceiling and began performing their acts while lights flashed in a colorful array to club-style music. Thankfully, the girls hurried back to the table with their drinks to watch the show.

James was furious, pacing the floor in his living room. His face clearly couldn't hide his displeasure with Michael and Samuel. "We are all going to sit down calmly and talk about this."

He stilled as the guys took a seat, then stepped in front of them. "Okay, let me get this straight. You met Annika and Callie from the States, who are here on vacation."

The guys nodded, one of them muttering something about sexy hot.

James pinched his brow and continued, "They're gorgeous young girls, and it's a given you'd be attracted to them."

"So? We meet girls all the time, and it never seemed to bother you before. What's different about these girls?" Michael shifted uncomfortably in the oversized chair he was seated on.

"I know Annika's mother," he calmly replied, struggling to maintain a hold on his emotions.

"Oh. Nothing happened. I swear it," Michael said.

"Samuel?" James moved to stand in front of his chair.

"Nothing. Not even a kiss. I swear," Samuel said.

"Good. That's what I wanted to hear. You both better be damn sure it's the truth." James sat down on the couch across from the boys. "No one so much as touches either one of them. Do I make myself clear?"

"Not a problem, Uncle," Michael said while Samuel nodded his agreement.

"Do you know where they are tonight?"

"Maybe Coco Bongo? Why?" Samuel asked.

"Damn it! Why would they go there?" James shouted.

"They asked what they should do while they were in Cancun, so we recommended it. Is that a problem?" Michael asked.

"You know who runs that place. Did you warn them it's not a safe place for tourists? Those girls would be prime targets for the Cartel. Particularly, Paulo and Diego. When I said no one touches them, I mean *no one*! Got that!"

"Okay. All you had to do was ask," Michael stated.

"You guys better find them. I want you two to spend every minute you can with them. Keep an eye on them. You'd better know where they are at all times. And absolutely no touching. Not even a kiss! Got it?"

Michael and Samuel nodded.

"Now get going! Let me know as soon as you find them."

During the intermission, the guys who struck up a conversation with the girls at the bar came over to the table to presumably pick up where they left off before the show started.

"Mom and Yvonne, this is Paulo and Diego," Annika said, introducing them.

"Welcome to Coco Bongo." Diego walked over to shake hands with Anna Marie and Yvonne.

"Do you work here?" Yvonne asked.

"My family owns it," Diego answered with a gleam in his eye. "Are you enjoying the show?"

"It's a bit loud in here, but the show has been entertaining," Anna Marie answered.

Paulo and Diego continued talking with the girls while Anna Marie and Yvonne watched. Thankfully, the intermission was soon over, and the lights lowered again, signaling that the second half of the show would begin. The guys excused themselves and went back to the bar.

"Paulo, good to see you, man." Michael shook his hand while Paulo signaled the bartender to bring them beers.

Diego walked up and shook his hand. "What brings you here tonight?" He nodded to Samuel but directed his question to Michael.

"Is it a crime to stop in to see our old friends?" Michael asked.

"Not at all. Good to see you, man. How long has it been?" Diego asked.

"A while." Michael scanned the crowd for the girls.

"Heard you were off to school. Flying planes, wasn't it?" Paulo asked.

"Yes." Michael kept his eyes focused on Diego.

The bartender set down two cans of Dos XX on the counter.

"Enjoy the show. Have some matters to attend to." Paulo and Diego glanced toward Annika and Callie as they walked away.

"Damn. That's not good." Michael realized they now had their work cut out for them as he sent James a text letting him know the girls were at Coco Bongo. Keeping Paulo and Diego away from the girls at this point wasn't going to be easy. In fact, none of it would be easy. Ever since James said no kissing, all he could think about was kissing Annika.

CHAPTER 8

AFTER THE SHOW WAS OVER, MICHAEL AND SAMUEL approached the girls at their table.

"Hello, everyone. How was the show? Did you enjoy it?" Michael fired off multiple questions.

"It was great. I love the Cirque de Soleil shows, and this Mexican version was excellent," Anna Marie answered while the others nodded their agreement.

"Were you here for the show, too?" Annika asked.

"We were out and thought maybe if you guys had chosen to go to the show tonight, we could give you a ride home so you wouldn't need to take the bus back." Michael smiled charmingly, hoping Anna Marie would trust him to get them safely back to The Royal Islander.

"That would be great! I, for one, am exhausted and would love not to have to take the bus," Yvonne stated.

Michael and Samuel escorted them outside, and Samuel excused himself to get the Suburban, which belonged to James. He insisted they take it since they would need the room to bring them all back to The Royal Islander. Assuming they found them.

Once back at the resort, they made their way to the pool bar.

"What would you ladies like to drink?" Samuel asked.

"Strawberry Daiquiri."

"Banana Monkey."

"Pina Colada."

"Mudslide."

They sat down at a table and waited while the guys ordered the drinks.

"So, what would you girls like to do tomorrow?" Yvonne asked.

"I kind of wanted to go snorkeling one day," Callie said.

"Me, too," Annika said.

Michael and Samuel set the drinks down and pulled up a couple of extra chairs. "I heard someone say something about snorkeling. We can take you out snorkeling, if you'd like. My uncle has a boat and we know all the best places to go."

"Really? What do you think, Mom?" Annika asked.

Anna Marie's expression appeared obviously doubtful.

"The invitation is for all four of you to come," Michael added.

"Yvonne?" Anna Marie asked.

"I'm game. Haven't been snorkeling in a long time."

"What about snorkeling equipment?" Anna Marie asked.

"It's free at the resort, just go down to the activity building in the morning and they will get you set up," Samuel offered.

"Mom, what do you say?" Annika asked.

"Okay, what time do you want us to be ready in the morning?" Anna Marie questioned.

"We can pick you up at eight. In front of the lobby," Samuel said.

After they finished their drinks, Anna Marie, Yvonne and the girls headed to their villa to get some much-needed rest for the big day tomorrow.

Michael didn't even attempt a hug and definitely wasn't about to even consider a good-bye kiss on the cheek. Just a simple wave, then he and Samuel walked toward the lobby. Unfortunately, now all he could think about was kissing Annika.

James heard the doorbell ring. He walked to the foyer, opened the door, and motioned for them to follow him into the living room.

After they were all seated, Michael said, "We found them up at Coco Bongo and gave them a ride back to The Royal Islander. They were trying to plan out what they wanted to do tomorrow, so we offered to take all four of the ladies out snorkeling on your boat for the whole day."

"You did what?" James asked.

"Well, we thought it was a good way to keep the girls out of trouble. You wanted us to keep an eye on them, right?"

James stood up and began pacing, then stopped at the window and stared out toward the ocean. "Right," he promptly answered.

"You said you knew Annika's mother, Anna Marie, so I thought you would want to come along anyway. Besides, you'd never let us take the boat without you."

James didn't even know what to say to that. No way in hell was he letting them take the boat. They were right about that. He hadn't planned on imposing himself on Anna Marie for the whole day, but this might work out to his benefit. She presumably wouldn't turn down the snorkeling excursion once they were on the boat. And she wouldn't know he was coming until they boarded the boat at the marina. Would she be able to spend the whole day without talking to him? That was the million-dollar question.

CHAPTER 9

"Annika, I'm not so sure we should be going on a boat with these young guys you just met. We virtually don't know anything about them. Maybe not the safest thing to be doing?" Anna Marie questioned.

"Well, I guess if we booked a tour guide, we wouldn't know who he was either," Yvonne offered.

"I guess you're right, let's get moving then. We only have half an hour until Michael and Samuel will be down in the lobby." Anna Marie headed to the bedroom to pack a bag.

They all scrambled to finish getting ready. Grabbing everything they thought they might need for the snorkeling outing, they rushed out the door.

Fifteen minutes later, they were at the sports desk getting fitted for their snorkeling gear.

"I'm done, so I'm going to the lobby to meet Michael and tell him you'll be coming shortly," Annika said, running toward the lobby. She arrived just in time to see Michael and Samuel pull up in a Suburban.

Michael got out and walked over to greet Annika. "How are you feeling on this bright sunny day in Cancun? Ready for a day on the water?"

"I'm so excited." Annika wondered why he'd stopped a couple of feet from her, but flashed him a bright smile to match his. She felt her body shift a little closer. A magnetic effect he had on her, apparently. She cautioned herself to remain steady, but it was a challenge considering how good he looked in his white t-shirt and black swim trunks. If she didn't know better, she'd have thought he was just a beach bum. A tall, extremely hot guy who towered above her. His dusty blond hair blew in the wind and was quickly raked back with strong fingers.

"Where's the rest of your group?" Michael glanced behind her.

"They'll be here any minute," she said just as the others appeared in the lobby.

"Great!" He held her gaze before turning to the group.

"Everyone ready to go?" Samuel got out and opened the door on his side to help them into the Suburban.

Thirty minutes later, they arrived at The Royal Marina, where the boat was docked. The marina housed many boats or *yachts*, which was clearly a better word. They followed Michael and Samuel down the long, narrow wooden dock to a beautiful yacht with the words, *Nordic Cruz*, displayed in large letters along the side.

The women were in awe. Minnesota had its share of boats, but they had never seen anything like this one—sleek, beautiful and definitely beckoning them to enjoy a day on its pristine white decks.

After they were all situated in seats, where they could see the turquoise waves gently lapping its sides and the shoreline's scenery of palm trees, the yacht effortlessly and smoothly glided away from the dock, leaving the marina behind them as it moved toward the open water.

Yvonne stood to look over the railing and take in the shoreline as they floated out to sea. Michael came to stand by her. "Who's driving the boat?" she asked him.

"Oh, my uncle James, of course. After all, it's his yacht. You can go up to the bridge, where he's steering, if you'd like to. There's an even better view from the bridge." Michael motioned toward the front of the yacht, then walked toward the rear in search of Annika.

Yvonne found her way to the bridge and saw a man at the helm of the yacht. He had his back toward her so she couldn't see his face. "Hi, I'm Yvonne," she said as the man turned around to greet her.

"Thomas Sandberg, nice to meet you."

"So, you're the *captain*, is that the correct word?" she asked, faltering, unsure if she used the correct term.

"No, that would be me, James Olson. And, you are Yvonne, I believe?" James said as he entered the bridge from a small room off to the right.

"Oh, my God! Anna Marie is going to be livid. Is this some kind of trick? Are you kidnapping us or something like that?" Yvonne exploded and stood in a defensive mode with her hands on her hips.

James walked closer in an effort to calm her down. "No, why don't you sit down, and we can talk about it?" He took her arm and guided her to a chair where she sat down. "Michael offered up my yacht to take the four of you out snorkeling without my knowledge or permission. There was no way I was going to let him take the yacht out alone, he's too young, so rather than have you ladies be disappointed, I offered that Thomas and I would come along to captain the yacht."

"This is bad," Yvonne said.

"Everything will be fine," James assured her.

"No, you don't understand. Annika and Callie have no idea that you and Anna Marie dated, much less that you even know each other. You have to act like you don't know her."

"That might be a bit awkward." James studied her face.

"First of all, Anna Marie doesn't want to speak to you, remember?" Yvonne questioned.

"Right. Small matter that needs to be resolved." James grinned.

"I agree, but this is unquestionably not the right way to go about it."

"Just for the record, I told Michael that I knew Anna Marie. Samuel doesn't know anything about Anna Marie and me knowing each other unless Michael told him. I suggest that we go out there so Michael can introduce me. I'll simply say I heard she was from Minnesota, mention that I went to Richfield High School, and she looks remarkably familiar to me..."

Yvonne stared at him in disbelief. Finally, she nodded. "Hope it works. I'll send Michael back here so you can fill him in." Yvonne left wondering what the outcome would be for this fateful day in Anna Marie's life.

Minutes later, James and Michael appeared in the rear of the boat. The ladies all turned to look at them.

Shock registered on Anna Marie's face, her hand went to her chest where her heart was, and she sat down on the nearest seat. Her mouth opened, but no words came out.

"I'd like to introduce you ladies to my Uncle James. This is his yacht that he so kindly offered to captain for our trip to Isla Mujeres. I know you are all from Minnesota and so is James."

James stared directly at Anna Marie. "I went to Richfield High School."

"My mom went to Richfield, too. Maybe you know each other?" Annika proudly stated for Anna Marie.

"That was a long time ago, when I was much younger." He laughed. "You do look somewhat familiar, Anna Marie. Although it was quite a large school back then, it was almost impossible to know everyone. People change. I'm sure we look much different than we did back then."

"Yes, that is true." Anna Marie eventually was able to speak, feeling somewhat relieved that he hadn't come right out and acknowledged he knew who she was in front of Annika.

"I need to tend to my captain duties. Want to get you all there safely." He started to leave, but then turned back slightly, "Nice to meet you, ladies. I look forward to spending this beautiful day with you."

"He seems like a nice guy. Extremely handsome for an old dude. What a coincidence that he's from Minnesota and you went to the same high school," Annika said while watching for her mother's reaction.

"Quite the coincidence." Anna Marie stared in the direction where James had made his timely exit.

Annika observed her mother with great interest. "Maybe you should go talk to him? Might make for an extremely interesting conversation about old high school times."

"Yes, why don't you go talk to him? He is awfully hot for an older guy," Yvonne prodded.

"I'm sure he's busy captaining the boat...or yacht, whatever this is. I have all day since it looks like he'll be spending the day with us."

Annika, Callie, Michael and Samuel opted for the lower deck, leaving Yvonne and Anna Marie on the main deck alone.

"What the hell was that all about?" Anna Marie asked.

"I think it went well considering everything." Yvonne shrugged her shoulders.

"What's that supposed to mean?"

"When Michael told me this was his Uncle James' boat, I wanted to be sure it wasn't *your* James he was talking about. I mean, what were the odds it would be *your* James? So, I went up to the bridge to check it out. And lo and behold, there stood *your* James."

"And you didn't say anything to me?" Anna Marie's face creased. "And he's not *my* James."

"I told James that Annika didn't know anything about him and you having dated. I think he did well, choosing his words very carefully."

"I guess so. I simply don't want to talk to him."

"I know, Anna Marie. Maybe you can just treat him like someone you just met for the first time today. Get to know the person he is now."

"I'll try. It's just that I've never loved anyone else besides him, and when I saw him, I wanted to slap his face for all the pain and heartbreak he caused me. I could've maybe forgotten him if it hadn't been for Annika. But she has always been a constant reminder of my love for James."

"Oh, Anna Marie." Yvonne moved to sit beside her. She put her arm around Anna Marie's shoulder. "I'm so sorry. I didn't realize you still cared about him all these years later."

"It was somehow easier thinking he'd died in the war. But now knowing he's alive, it's so much harder."

"That's why I think you should talk to him. He has no idea he is a father, right?" Yvonne asked.

"I never heard from him after he left. How could I tell him?" Anna Marie questioned.

"Did you ever try to find him?"

"No, back then, it wasn't so easy to try to track someone down. Now that the internet exists, it's probably doable. After he broke up with me, I sent him a letter and told him I never wanted to see him again. He was supposed to know that when someone says that, they're hurt and don't mean it literally. Then, when I didn't hear from him, I was so angry, and I felt like I just wasn't good enough. I figured he either died or found someone new, so I didn't try."

"Well, he's right here, right now." Yvonne smiled.

"I know I told him I never wanted to see him again, but he should've known better. He should've known I wanted him to come back." Anna Marie gazed out at what seemed a never-ending ocean.

"Guys aren't the smartest when it comes to deciphering what we actually mean when we say something. Maybe he was simply honoring your wishes?"

"I'll think about talking to him like you said, as a person I just met. I'm definitely not going to mention anything about Annika yet. Before I do that, I need to have a conversation with her about this whole situation first. At least I think I should tell her before him. What do you think?" she asked.

Yvonne appeared deep in thought. "You got me there. Not sure who would be the best to tell first. In the end, it just comes down to both of them knowing."

"Right. What a mess! I came down here to relax and have some fun with Annika. Not sure that's what's happening at all." Anna Marie brushed away a strand of hair from her face.

"It can still be fun. Have faith. This may be the best unexpected thing to happen to you both."

The group watched as James pulled up to the Manchones Reef, part of the Mesoamerican Barrier Reef, which was thirty feet deep, where multiple boats were anchored. They heard the anchor release as it lowered into the water, and the engine stopped. James took a deep breath in anticipation of seeing Anna Marie again, hoping she had calmed down by now. Hoping she would simply talk to him.

Michael, Samuel and the girls were busy shedding clothes and putting on their snorkeling gear, including life jackets, when James and Thomas appeared in the rear of the yacht.

Yvonne and Anna Marie were observing but not preparing to go into the water.

"I had presumed you ladies were going snorkeling, too." James looked from Anna Marie to Yvonne.

"I haven't been snorkeling for years, not sure I remember what you're supposed to do. I can stay on the yacht." Anna Marie sat back down.

"You ladies are wearing swimsuits, I presume, and brought snorkeling gear, right?" James asked.

"James and I can assist you if you'd like," Thomas offered. "We've been snorkeling and scuba diving for years."

"I'd feel better if you both came along," Yvonne said and looked to Anna Marie for her agreement.

"Yes, I'd feel safer then," Anna Marie immediately said, not wanting to miss the opportunity to see the Manchones National Park, home to over 500 fish species, even if she needed James to come along so she wouldn't be afraid. Besides, she wouldn't have to talk to him with a snorkel in her mouth.

"Excellent. We'll go change and be back in a few minutes. That'll give you ladies time to get ready," Thomas said.

James and Thomas climbed the stairs to the bridge.

Anna Marie didn't speak as she was lost in her own thoughts. Wondering if James would still find her attractive in a bikini after all these years. She took off her beach cover-up and put her hair up in a ponytail. She knew Yvonne was waiting for her to say something. "I'll be fine. We're all adults here. I can make this work."

"Good thing you absolutely want to see the Great Mayan Reef, or you assuredly wouldn't have even given it a shot." Yvonne picked up her life jacket and put it on. She stood by the railing waiting for the men to return, holding her snorkel, mask and flippers in her hand.

Anna Marie did the same and joined Yvonne, just as James and Thomas came down the steps.

James couldn't tear his eyes from Anna Marie. He appreciated the vision presented before him, in fact, she looked just as he remembered her in a bikini all those years ago at the beach on Lake Harriet back in Minnesota. He only looked away when Thomas began going over the snorkeling basics for them. Everyone put on their flippers and descended the ladder. Once they reached the water, they put on their masks and placed the snorkels in their mouths. Thomas went first, then Yvonne, next Anna Marie and James last. This was the order Thomas had stated they should stay in if possible, so he could lead them, and James would be able to observe them from the rear in case anyone needed help.

Below them lay a beautiful array of colors, filled with schools of Grunts, Sergeant Majors, Damselfish, French Angelfish, colorful Parrotfish, and nature in progress.

They caught up with Annika, Callie, Michael and Samuel, finally stopping to take a break as they floated in the warm Gulf of Mexico waters, exclaiming about the fish they'd seen and the beautiful elkhorn coral.

A couple of hours later, they returned to the yacht, climbing the ladder back onto the deck, pulling off the mask, snorkel and flippers on the way up. James went up first so he could assist everyone getting off the ladder onto the rear deck.

After they were all on the deck once again and collapsed on the seats, James asked, "Anyone hungry?"

"Starving," they all replied and began laughing.

"Thomas, let's get underway and dock in town, so we can all get some food," James said as he and Thomas made their way to the bridge.

The ladies took turns changing into shorts and tank tops in the yacht's small bathroom. Then the guys changed. Before long, they were docking at Puerto Isla Mujeres Resort and Yacht Club. Once the yacht was tied and secured to the dock, Thomas helped them step out of the yacht one by one. Michael and Samuel escorted the girls down the waterfront to the Yacht Club restaurant.

Thomas struck up a conversation with Yvonne as they headed down the dock, leaving Anna Marie to walk with James.

"So, did you have fun snorkeling, Anna Marie?" James asked as they strolled down the dock.

"Yes, it was a new experience for me snorkeling in the ocean." Anna Marie slowed down her pace to walk beside him.

"Good. I was hoping it wouldn't be too awkward for you to be with me." James smiled.

"It's okay, it wasn't your fault we ended up in this predicament."

"We do need to talk, but I'd like to do it when we can have some privacy. What needs to be said is between you and me only." James stopped walking to face her.

"I agree," Anna Marie said.

"I'd like to take you to dinner and then we can find a quiet private place to talk afterwards, if that would be okay with you?" James couldn't believe how nervous he felt. His heart was thumping in his chest.

"Fine, I'll agree to that." Anna Marie studied his handsome face.

"Wednesday?" James asked.

Anna Marie hesitated for a moment, showing her uncertainty. Finally, she answered, staring intently into his eyes. "Okay." She then turned and walked towards the waiting group ahead of them.

CHAPTER 10

ANNA MARIE ENTERED THE YACHT CLUB RESTAURANT WITH James' arm gently surrounding her back to guide her through the doorway. It had been years since he'd been with her, but it felt so natural. This was his first meal with her in over twenty years. So, he sure as hell would try his best to enjoy every minute he had with her.

The conversation centered on the Mesoamerican Barrier Reef that they'd seen while snorkeling and, of course, all the colorful fish. Their group was seated at a large table, complete with a full view of the ocean. Before long, the table was filled with appetizers, food and wine.

"So, if it's not too brash to ask, what do you do? For your job, I mean." Yvonne asked, catching James' attention.

"I work in the tourist and hotel industry here in Cancun," James said, trying his hardest not to tell the whole truth, but not to lie either. He gave Michael, Samuel, and Thomas the look, telling them not to say anything regarding the subject.

"You don't live in the US anymore, then?" Annika asked.

"I have dual citizenship with the US and Mexico. I have a home in Cancun and one in Denver."

"Wow, you must be quite wealthy," Callie stated.

"I do okay. How about you girls? Are you in college?" James redirected the conversation toward the girls.

"We just graduated from Concordia College a few weeks ago. This trip is to celebrate making it through four years of college." Annika glanced across the table at Michael and Samuel.

"Here's to graduating from college." Michael lifted his glass in a toast to Annika's wine glass.

"So, what are your plans for the future now that you've graduated?" James asked the girls.

"Not sure yet. When we get back home, I'll be waiting to hear back about the applications I submitted for marketing internships. Hopefully, I will get a job offer so I can start paying back the rest of my student loans." Annika smiled his way.

"I'm sure you'll find one," James offered.

After finishing every bit of the food on the table, including multiple desserts of Tres Leches Cake, Churros, Concha, Flan and Fried Ice Cream that James ordered for everyone to share, they were ready to head back to the resort.

When the waiter came by, James handed her a black American Express card. "I got this."

"But you don't have to, we can pay for our part," Anna Marie offered.

"It's my treat. I had a memorable day with you, lovely ladies."

As they walked back to the yacht, the sun was nearing the horizon. James noticed the Sangria yacht docked near them. He looked around to see if anyone was watching them. Diego Sanchez's father owned that particular yacht, which meant Diego had either followed them, or it was just a coincidence that both yachts were in Isla Mujeres today. Most of all, it meant trouble. Diego had always been trouble, and once he decided he wanted a girl, he would try to get her one way or the other. James didn't want to entertain the idea that these girls could be the next target, but seeing the boat moored next to his made his neck prickle.

On the way back to Cancun, everyone sat in the rear of the yacht except for James and Thomas, who were on the bridge. James kept pacing the floor, what little of it there was. To say he was pissed would be putting it mildly. If Diego laid a hand on Annika, he might have to take matters into his own hands.

Later, after the yacht had been docked in Cancun, they walked to where the Suburban was parked. Michael and Samuel took the front seats, while the girls got into the third-row seat.

Yvonne and Anna Marie took the back seats. She powered down the window. They were finally ready to head back to The Royal Islander.

James stood outside the window on Anna Marie's side, waiting. "What are your plans for tomorrow?" he asked.

"We were going to rent a car and drive to Playa del Carmen," Anna Marie explained. "Then take the ferry across to Cozumel."

"Let me arrange a shuttle bus to take you," James offered. "It will be more comfortable and you'll feel safer if you don't have to drive down to Playa del Carmen with all the crazy drivers. It's not like driving in the States. I'll have the shuttle pick you up at nine."

"Won't that be expensive?" Anna Marie asked.

"I know people down here. Let me take care of it for you." He looked at her with pleading eyes.

"If you insist. I wasn't looking forward to driving. It looks kind of scary. Thanks." Anna Marie stared into his eyes.

Yvonne leaned over toward the window to say, "Thanks for everything you did for us today."

"Thanks," Annika added.

"Thanks," Callie said.

"Yes, thanks for a wonderful day," Anna Marie said, flashing him an unexpected, genuine smile of gratitude.

James backed away from the Suburban as it pulled out of the parking lot. Damn, he'd unquestionably wanted to kiss her when she'd bestowed him with that smile of hers. She'd softened to him over the course of the day, and it was stirring up feelings he thought he'd overcome long ago. Sleeping wouldn't come easily tonight, that was for sure.

CHAPTER 11

NEXT DAY

"Everyone ready?" Callie called out.

"I think we have everything we need for the day." Yvonne grabbed her large bag and followed Callie out the door.

"We're coming," Anna Marie said as she and Annika followed them out the door.

A luxurious mini tour bus pulled up at the entrance promptly at nine. Anna Marie was a bit surprised. "Pretty fancy for a shuttle bus."

"You must be Anna Marie, Yvonne, Annika and Callie," the driver stated after stepping out.

"Yes," Annika said, speaking for all of them.

"I'm Pedro. I'm here to take you to Playa Del Carmen, correct?" he asked.

"Yes!" Callie replied.

"And you want to catch the eleven o'clock ferry to Cozumel, correct?" he asked.

"Yes, that won't be a problem, will it?" Anna Marie asked.

"No, madam. I will take care of everything." He motioned for them to board, helping them as they stepped inside and took their seats.

Anna Marie and Yvonne sat together, and the girls sat behind them.

"What do you girls want to do in Cozumel?" Anna Marie asked.

"Walk around the main streets and go shopping. Have a drink. Have lunch overlooking the ocean." Annika waved her arms around them to accentuate her words.

"Yes! That all sounds fun!" Callie chimed in.

They arrived at the ferry dock thirty minutes early.

Pedro pulled up to the ticket booth, and they all stepped out of the bus. "Ladies, please wait here, and I will get your tickets."

Anna Marie attempted to object and say they could get their own tickets, but he had already turned and walked away. "Well, I guess we can just pay him for the tickets when he gets back."

"Mom, I'm thinking that James is covering it for you. In fact, I think he likes you." Annika laughed.

"Don't be silly. He's just being nice." Anna Marie turned away to walk over to Yvonne.

"Right, Mom." Annika smiled.

The girls strolled over to the pier to look around while they waited.

Yvonne shook her head. "Did you truthfully think they wouldn't notice the way he looks at you?"

"I have no idea what you're talking about. He's reasonably just shocked to see me again after all these years, and like I just said, he's just being nice." Anna Marie tilted her head and smiled.

"Right. Just keep telling yourself that." Yvonne gave her the look.

"Whatever." Anna Marie glanced over toward the girls. If they could tell he was interested, they'd surely be able to tell something was or had been going on between her and James. She needed to figure out what she was going to do and how she felt about him. The sooner the better!

"This may be your second chance at love with James," Yvonne said as she displayed a huge grin.

"Just to be clear, I haven't thought about him for years. In fact, I never thought I'd see him again. Ever!" What a lie! She'd never stopped thinking about him.

Minutes later, Pedro walked back to where they were waiting on the pier and handed Anna Marie the ferry tickets.

"Thank you." She took the tickets and handed one to each of the girls and Yvonne.

The ferry's horn signaled loudly as it neared the dock. After the ship was secured, the people on board disembarked.

"I'll pick you up at seven-thirty tonight, right here at the dock," Pedro informed them. "The ferry leaves Cozumel to return at six and arrives back in Playa del Carmen at six forty-five. That will give you some time for a little shopping."

"Yes, that'll be great. Thank you so much for all your help." Anna Marie replied with a smile.

Pedro nodded and turned to walk back to the shuttle bus.

Anna Marie joined the girls and Yvonne, who were waving to her from the line waiting to board the ferry.

Onboard, they found seats by the window and watched Playa del Carmen's shoreline disappear into the horizon.

"What's the plan once we get to Cozumel?" Annika asked.

"I guess we never made a decision on that. What does everyone want to do?" Anna Marie threw out there.

"Shop!" Annika replied.

"Eat!" Callie added.

"I hear that you can rent bicycles to tour the island," Yvonne stated.

"Or scooters, or we could rent a jeep and drive around the island," Annika added.

～

Forty minutes later, the ferry arrived at the Cozumel dock. They all headed down the main street where they'd decided to do whichever option came up first. As they turned the corner, a row of jeeps came into view, so it appeared that they would be using the jeep rental option.

"We have to see how much it costs first," Anna Marie said as she walked up to the counter.

"Hello, ladies. My name is Arthur and I have a special today for the jeep tour. We had a cancellation, so I will give you a good deal. If you sign up now, it will only be $25 per person. We are leaving in 10 minutes, though." Arthur waited for their answer.

Anna Marie looked from Annika to Callie to Yvonne.

They all nodded their approval.

Yvonne and Anna Marie handed Arthur their credit cards to pay, and before they knew it, they were all seated in the jeep waiting to follow close behind the jeep in front of them. It was a picture-perfect day with clear blue skies and bright sunshine. The wheels started rolling, and soon the jeep tour was on the move with their hair blowing wildly in the wind. Yvonne had opted to be the driver since she was the only one who knew how to drive a stick shift, which meant Anna Marie could sit back and enjoy the ride.

The tour included a stop at a beach on the other side of the island, where lunch would be served and snorkeling was an option. Anna Marie felt a bit relieved to be part of a tour, so they didn't have to figure out where to go on their own. All they had to do was follow the jeep ahead of them and stop when the group stopped. Lunch was delicious, home-made tacos prepared on a private beach under a tent. The girls opted to take advantage of the snorkeling while Anna Marie and Yvonne decided to lounge in the chairs on the beach.

At last, Anna Marie had some time to herself to ponder the situation with James. She'd been angry at him for so many years, which made it hard to be around him now. Especially when he was being overly friendly to her. Had he regretted not returning to her after he was discharged from the Army? They'd both been so young then.

The attraction was definitely still there. She couldn't deny it. The question was, did he feel it too? And if he did, would he feel the same way after he found out Annika was his daughter? Many questions she didn't have answers to.

Would she be willing to let him back into her life? She watched her daughter walk back from the ocean across the white sand, water dripping from her body, a massive smile on her face. What would Annika's reaction be to finding out James was her dad?

Promptly at three, the jeep tour returned to downtown Cozumel. Now it was time to, *Shop till you Drop*, looking for deals and things, they most likely didn't need. But of course, it was the thrill of the hunt to find something truly unique. After purchasing tank tops with Cozumel printed on them and a few other must-haves, they stood in line waiting for the ferry.

The return ride back to Playa del Carmen was relaxing after a day in the sun. They'd decided to have dinner quickly in Playa del Carmen before Pedro arrived to pick them up.

After the ferry docked, they hurried off the ship.

Surprisingly, they saw Michael and Samuel standing on the corner. The girls picked up the pace and walked even faster toward them.

"What are you doing here?" Annika asked, smiling at Michael.

"Heard there were a couple of gorgeous ladies who would be getting off the ferry around seven." Michael grinned.

"Hello, Michael. Samuel." Anna Marie walked over to them.

Samuel and Callie appeared to be in deep conversation, but Yvonne had no qualms about interrupting them. "Hello, Samuel."

At this, the boys directed their attention to the mothers. "Playa has some of the best restaurants around. We would love to take you all to dinner before you go back to Cancun," Michael stated.

"But Pedro is picking us up at seven-thirty," Yvonne countered.

"Oh, we came instead of Pedro," Michael said. "We'll be giving you a ride back to Cancun in the Suburban. If that's alright?"

Anna Marie was a bit hesitant to agree. These boys kept showing up, infusing themselves into their plans.

"Mom?" Annika gave Anna Marie her pleading look.

The girls were obviously delighted with the attention.

"Well, we do need to eat something for supper. So, where's this restaurant?" Anna Marie asked.

"It's only a couple of blocks away. It's a nice night for a walk. Or we can drive?" Samuel offered.

Anna Marie looked toward Yvonne, who smiled, which meant she knew there was only one choice. The girls wanted to do this, so they would do it. "We can walk."

"Great! Follow me." Michael pointed toward the main street as he headed away, and the rest of the group followed.

Annika walked beside Michael, Callie with Samuel. Yvonne and Anna Marie followed behind them.

"I think the girls like these boys. Maybe a little too much," Yvonne whispered.

"I think you may be right," Anna Marie agreed.

CHAPTER 12

MICHAEL STOPPED AT THE PLANK RESTAURANT. THEY ALL
followed him inside. Nautical items adorned the walls. Fish nets,
glass globe lights, and old maps of the area. He conversed in Spanish
with the pretty Latina hostess.

She nodded to the group, picked up English menus and led them
upstairs to a table overlooking the famous 5th Avenue and the
Caribbean Sea, which was part of the Atlantic Ocean. An ocean blue
tablecloth covered the table, set nicely with glasses rimmed in blue
and silverware wrapped in white linen napkins.

On one side of the room was a black-laminated bar where two
well-dressed men were seated, facing it, holding drinks in front of
them.

Anna Marie knew she was staring, but she couldn't help it. Was
that really James and Thomas? She sat down in her chair just as the
men turned, stood and walked towards her. Of course, it would be
them!

"Ladies, hope you enjoyed your day in Cozumel," James said as
he stopped next to Anna Marie's chair.

There was no denying time had been good to him. His deeply tanned chest was conveniently on display through the open buttons at the top of his shirt.

Why did he have to look so attractive? Her thoughts were quickly interrupted.

"We had a great time," Callie said.

"It looks like we have a couple of empty chairs. Would you like to join us?" Annika said, smiling at James.

James nodded to Thomas. "We wouldn't want to impose on your group."

"Don't be silly, join us," Yvonne said.

James looked directly at Anna Marie as if waiting for her approval.

She'd seen the way Annika looked at James. It was almost like they had this natural, friendly manner between them. *Little did they know.* She obviously didn't have any choice but to agree.

"Yes, please join us." She looked up directly into his eyes that had haunted her dreams for way too many years. Unfortunately, she assumed they would take their seats at the other end of the table where the empty chairs were located, but Michael and Samuel stood up and moved to the empty chairs so Thomas and James could sit next to Yvonne and her.

She knew she needed to get a grip and go with the flow, as they say. If only her heart would slow down to its normal beating rate! And hopefully soon. She took a deep breath in and exhaled slowly. She was a big girl, she could do this.

Thankfully, the waiter arrived to take their drink orders. She was first and ordered a glass of blush wine. James was last. He ordered a glass of an exceptionally expensive red wine and told the waiter they would only need one check. The waiter nodded and walked away.

Only minutes later, the waiter returned with their drinks, then proceeded to take their food orders.

Anna Marie ordered salmon, Yvonne ordered snapper, and the

girls ordered Mexican Fajitas. Thomas and James ordered the catch of the day—Blue Marlin. Michael and Samuel decided on fish tacos.

"So, what did you do in Cozumel today?" James asked her.

"I guess you'd call it souvenir shopping. Mainly for T-shirts that said Cozumel on them." Anna Marie laughed.

"I hear ladies love shopping." Thomas grinned.

"Not going to deny that. But we did go on a jeep tour to the other side of the island, which was fun," Yvonne stated.

"Yes, and Yvonne did an excellent job driving," Anna Marie added.

"That's because I'm the only one who knows how to drive a stick. Even though it's been a while, I think I did a pretty good job. Thankfully, it was only a two-lane road and not a freeway!" Yvonne laughed.

"You did great!" Anna Marie said.

"Sometimes I think we spend more time flying than driving." Yvonne smiled toward Anna Marie.

"So, you ladies work for the airlines?" Thomas asked.

"Yes, we work for Champion Air, which is a charter air company that services vacation packages for MLT Vacations in Minneapolis." Anna Marie took a sip of her wine.

"What do you do at Champion Air?" James asked.

"Oh, we're flight attendants. We've been there for 20 years, so with our seniority, it allows us the best choice of flights to work, which has been a godsend for us as single moms," Yvonne offered.

Anna Marie couldn't believe Yvonne had just given out all that information in just two short sentences. And to James of all people, especially when she didn't know anything about what he'd been doing all these years. She was about to ask him when dinner arrived.

The conversation shifted to the delicious food they were eating, so she never had the opportunity to ask her question.

After clearing their dinner plates, she observed James say something softly to the waiter. Soon, he returned with a tray of Mexican ice cream drizzled with chocolate and a few slices of strawberries on the side of each plate.

Anna Marie took a bite of hers, biting into the crispy, warm coating filled with cold vanilla ice cream inside. She had no clue how they managed to deep fry them without the ice cream totally melting. All she knew was they were scrumptious.

With the dessert dishes cleared, James stood, pushing his chair back. "It's a bit of a drive back to Cancun, so we should get you ladies back to The Royal Islander. I'm sure you potentially already have another busy day planned for tomorrow."

Annika looked his way. "We're going on the jet boats across from the hotel for the Jungle tour and snorkeling. I'm so excited, it should be a lot of fun."

They all stood and followed James out of the restaurant to 5th Avenue. Once everyone was down on the street, James made a suggestion. "We have both my and Thomas' Suburbans here. They only hold six passengers. So, I'd like to propose taking Anna Marie, Annika and Michael back in mine, and Thomas can take Yvonne, Callie and Samuel. It's an hour ride, so this way it won't be so crowded. Or you ladies can ride with Michael and Samuel back in one of the cars, and Thomas and I will take the other one back."

Anna Marie looked over at Yvonne, knowing Yvonne would choose to ride back with Thomas.

Seeing Anna Marie's dilemma, Yvonne suggested, "How about the four adults ride back together in one car and the young people can take the other one?"

Anna Marie knew they were all waiting for her to pick one of the options, she could feel their eyes on her. This wasn't fair! Finally, she said, "I think the four of us adults should ride together."

Annika clapped her hands and exclaimed, "Thanks, Mom." She ran over and hugged her while whispering in her ear, "Don't worry. We'll be fine."

The group walked down the tourist-filled street to where two Suburbans were parked. Both vehicles were midnight black, with tinted windows and matching plates—RR-1 and RR-2. It seemed odd, but then again, she had no idea how Mexico did its license plates. James opened the front passenger door and motioned for her to get in.

Oh well, surely didn't matter where she sat, she was just glad to have Yvonne and Thomas there, so maybe they could carry on the conversation, or it might be a very quiet ride back. She reluctantly stepped up into the Suburban, and soon they were headed back to Cancun.

Since it was still light out, James made small talk, pointing out places along the way back with Thomas and Yvonne carrying the rest of the conversation, mostly about places they'd traveled to.

Finally, they arrived back at The Royal Islander. James stepped out to open the door for her, taking her hand to help her out.

Anna Marie had no idea what a simple touch of his hand would do to her. Instantly, she felt the warmth from his hand, and as she stepped down, her proximity to James became only inches. The spicy fragrance of his aftershave was intoxicating to say the least. She was so close to his chest, staring into those baby blue eyes that had been her undoing so many years ago. Her mind raced to his lips and what it would be like to kiss him just one more time.

At that moment, they both realized Thomas and Yvonne were waiting a few feet away on the curb. James backed up and released her hand. She looked away and walked over to Yvonne.

"Remember, dinner tomorrow night. Seven?" James asked.

"Yes," Anna Marie replied in a shaky voice.

"I'll pick you up here. See you tomorrow for dinner," he added as he walked back to the car.

"I guess, I'm leaving." Thomas grinned and got in the car.

Anna Marie and Yvonne watched the Suburban drive away.

"What just happened?" Yvonne asked.

"Don't ask," Anna Marie quipped with just a little bit of snarkiness.

"Dinner?" Yvonne stared at her.

Anna Marie didn't give her an answer.

A few minutes later, the other Suburban pulled up with their daughters.

CHAPTER 13

"Did you enjoy today, Annika?" Anna Marie asked as they waited for the elevator, which would take them to their penthouse villa.

"I positively did! We were talking with the boys about staying in touch once we get back to the States. Callie and I have no idea where we'll end up yet. But it could possibly be the same places."

"Wow, you must really like him?" Anna Marie asked.

"He's so smart. He knows so much about aeronautics." Annika beamed.

Anna Marie loved seeing her daughter happy. "What kind of job is he looking for?"

"They're both trying to get in with a major airline in the US. If they do, they'll be able to fly anywhere, so meeting up is totally doable." Happy anticipation radiated through Annika.

Once in their villa, everyone changed into their PJs, and the girls were off to their room to watch TV in bed.

Anna Marie and Yvonne relaxed on the sofa in the living room.

"Ok, so tell me when this whole going to dinner conversation happened?" Yvonne asked.

"I told him on the yacht on our way to Isla Mujeres that I would meet him for dinner on Wednesday. I'm regretting it now. I don't know if I can do it," Anna Marie confessed.

"Why not? You two seemed to be getting along?" Yvonne questioned.

"I don't know what's going on with me. Apparently, it's been way too long since I went out with a man. Any man. I actually was thinking about what it would be like to kiss him one more time when he helped me out of the Suburban." Anna Marie stood up and soon was pacing in front of the patio doors. "We were way too close to each other."

"Oh...but he's picking you up at seven," Yvonne concluded.

"Unless, I cancel." Anna Marie stopped pacing abruptly.

"I don't think that's a good idea. You two need to talk," Yvonne said. "Not so sure kissing should be a part of it, but you do need to talk to him."

"I'm going to sleep now so I can stop thinking about this whole situation I've found myself in." Anna Marie slowly made her way to the bedroom.

Everyone was up at eight to shower and get ready for the day. First was breakfast at Captain Cove's across the street. They would need to wear swimsuits with cover-ups and bring towels along for their Jungle Tour, that was just a block away from the restaurant. The weather had been great, and they'd woken up to another day filled with bright sunshine and a temp of 85.

The hostess led them to a table overlooking the Lagoon.

"I'm so excited to drive the jet boats, Mom," Annika said.

"Do you want to go with me, or do you and Callie want to go together?" Anna Marie asked.

"I want to go with you," Annika said. "But can I drive? Please."

"I have no desire to drive, so sure," Anna Marie said.

"Should we do the breakfast buffet or do you want to order off the menu?" Yvonne asked.

It was unanimous for the buffet, so they all headed up to fill their plates. So much food!

Promptly at ten, they walked into the Jungle Tour office. They were fitted for their snorkeling gear and life jackets, then went outside to wait for the tour to start.

All the boats were a bright yellow color with a different number on the back of each one. They were directed to their assigned boats, where they climbed in and took their seats. After a few instructions on how to operate the boats, their instructor moved on to the next boat lined up beside the dock.

It became a follow-the-leader tour, so all the boats left one by one, leaving a large gap between them. The tour was a meandering path through mangrove channels lined with skinny islands, each with lush green canopy trees. Once through them, they entered an area where the lagoon met the ocean. Underneath lay a small coral reef. The boats were beached on one of the island's shores, and then they walked into the shallow water to snorkel. The varieties of fish—Parrotfish and Angelfish—with their bright tropical colors were surreal. Like nothing they'd ever seen before. Especially not in Minnesota.

Before they knew it, they were tying the boats back up at the dock where they'd started. After they'd turned in the snorkel equipment, they went over to see the photos taken of them on their adventure today.

"These are great! Mom, look," Annika said.

How could they not buy a couple? Action photos of her and her daughter. A once-in-a-lifetime experience for them both. "Which ones do you like best? Pick out a couple to get."

"Look at these, Annika!" Callie said, pulling her over to look.

"Hard to believe alligators live in that water," the clerk said.

"Really glad I wasn't actually aware of that when we were out there!" Callie exclaimed.

Yvonne and Anna Marie paid for the picture packages, and they all headed back to the resort.

"How're you doing?" Yvonne walked beside Anna Marie.

"I'm getting nervous. Should I cancel? I think I should cancel, right?" Anna Marie questioned.

"No. You need to go. It'll be all right. Simply catching up on the last twenty-plus years between two old friends," Yvonne stated.

"I can't tell him, but I can't lie either. Maybe I can do the half-truth, not the whole truth thing?" she asked.

"Once you're there, just do whatever feels right at that time," Yvonne suggested.

Back at the resort, they all went for a refreshing swim and dried off by relaxing in a pool chaise. Mostly on Anna Marie's mind was cancelling or postponing the dinner. Deep down, though, she knew she had to do it. When she'd watched James and Annika talking and saw the natural way they reacted to each other, she knew she owed it to Annika. She had a right to know and make her own decisions regarding James. On the other hand, she didn't realistically feel she owed anything to him. He gave up his rights by choosing not to return to Minnesota.

Around five, she got up to go back to the room to shower and change. At this point, it was simply something that needed to be done. What happened, happened. No more worrying about it.

She'd just stepped out of the shower and dried off when someone knocked on the door.

"Mom, can I come in?" Annika asked.

Anna Marie pulled a robe on and walked over to open the door.

"I just heard from Yvonne that you're having dinner with James. I think that's great! You didn't say anything to me about it, so I'm hoping you don't think that I'd have a problem with it, do you?" Annika asked.

"No, why would you think that?" Anna Marie asked.

"I know you haven't dated for a long time, and I kind of feel like it was because of me. That you felt I needed all of your attention. I'm going to be off finding my own path in life, and I want you to do the same. Don't get me wrong, I loved it just being the two of us. Sometimes I wonder what it would've been like to have a father, but I guess it just wasn't in the cards. I want you to find someone to spend your life with. Travel the world. Take you out to dinner and love you as much as I do. You deserve it. James is an extremely handsome older man who genuinely appears to like you. So let me help you get ready so you can wow him! You never know what will happen. Remember, he has a place in the States, too."

Anna Marie was at a loss for words. If Annika only knew how heavy her heart felt in anticipation of this dinner. But her words rang true. She'd given her life to raising her daughter, and now it was her turn to get out there and find someone she could love again. She didn't want to shatter Annika's dreams of that someone being James, because that wasn't going to happen.

If she were able to open her heart to love again, it certainly wouldn't be to the one person who'd shattered her heart and dreams into a million pieces. A kiss could tell a lot, and maybe she could have just one little kiss. Then she could be sure she didn't still love him after all these years.

At five to seven, she walked out to the resort entrance in her little black dress and four-inch heels, to find him waiting patiently for her arrival.

CHAPTER 14

JAMES SPENT THE DAY REHEARSING IN HIS MIND WHAT HE would say to Anna Marie, but unfortunately, nothing seemed right. Where did he even start? Presumably, the beginning would be the best place. He'd been young, and there were no excuses for breaking her heart. When he'd realized he'd made an enormous mistake more than five years later, he'd assumed she'd forgotten all about him and moved on. So, what would've been the point? His dad had been transferred to Denver shortly after he'd left for the Army, so he'd never made the trip back to Minneapolis.

Should he tell her he still thought about her?

Then she stepped through the automatic opening glass doors. He saw those long tan legs in heels with a short black dress that clung to her body like a second skin. She'd definitely dressed to show him what he'd been missing out on all these years. If there was any way to make this whole situation right with her, he was going to find it. He wanted a second chance at the life he'd walked away from with her by his side.

"You look breathtaking," he said, walking up to her, taking her hand to help her into his Suburban.

"Thank you." Anna Marie took his hand and stepped into the car. "So where are we going?" she asked after he got into the vehicle.

"Just down the street. Fred's Seafood Restaurant, a favorite of mine," he answered.

He turned on a station playing songs from the eighties and proceeded to exit onto the road.

After a quick ride in silence, listening to the music, he pulled into Fred's parking lot.

The hostess greeted them at the door. "Just follow me this way." She led them to a beautifully decorated patio overlooking the Lagoon, where a few other couples were already seated.

James pulled out the chair for her like a perfect gentleman, then took his seat across the table from Anna Marie.

The hostess handed them menus and left.

Primo California Stag's Leap white Chardonnay sat chilling in ice. The waiter arrived quickly and filled their glasses.

"They're known for their fish," James said. "But the steaks are great, too."

Anna Marie continued to scan the menu, but didn't say anything, except for nodding.

The waiter returned, and James ordered Lobster Bisque soup and Surf and Turf—Lobster and Filet Mignon—with a baked potato and sautéed vegetables.

Anna Marie waited patiently, and when the waiter turned to take her order, she said, "I'll have the same."

The waiter left and returned with a bread basket.

"I'm glad you agreed to have dinner with me, Anna Marie." James looked into her eyes, searching for some way to understand what she was thinking. He picked up a roll and buttered it.

"I'm not sure what you want to talk about?" she asked.

"Okay, that's fair. First, I want to tell you how sorry I am for the way I handled telling you I'd joined the Army." James watched her reaction.

"Really? That's what you're sorry about?" she questioned.

James hadn't expected that reaction. "I loved you, Anna Marie, that hadn't changed."

"We could've worked it out together. I could've gone with you." A tear almost appeared.

He could see great sadness in her eyes. "You were registered for Normandale College, and I didn't want to take that away from you. You worked so hard to get that opportunity."

"I loved you, James. I thought we'd made *love* that night before you left. I thought you were going to propose to me that night. I had already started planning our wedding in my head." Anna Marie bared her soul to him.

"I had no idea." James was at a loss for words.

"We talked about it." She stared at him. "Our friends were all engaged."

He now realized how deeply he'd hurt her. "Anna Marie, I'm so sorry."

"Did you get my letter?" Unshed tears pooled in her eyes, as she desperately willed them not to fall to her cheeks.

"My mother got it right before they moved and packed it in a box with my stuff. By the time I came back home two years later, she'd forgotten about it, and I didn't unpack my boxes until I got my own place more than four years later. After I read it, I felt there was no going back, because you certainly hated me even more by then."

Anna Marie only said two words. "I see."

The waiter set the Lobster Bisques in front of them and left.

Anna Marie held back the tears and raised a spoonful to her mouth. "So, tell me what you did after the military."

"My goal for the Army was to learn how to fly airplanes, so after I got out, I applied with Continental Airlines. I was then hired to fly the commuter jets and worked my way up the ladder to the Boeing 747 International flights. I was based in Denver, so I have a residence there."

"Looks like all your dreams came true."

"I wouldn't say that. How about you? What did you do?" He then took a spoonful of the creamy soup.

"It took a few years to get all my credits to graduate from Normandale, since I had to work to pay for the classes, I could only go part-time. Afterwards, I took Travel Agent Education classes and got a job with MLT Vacations."

"I thought I heard Yvonne say you both were flight attendants?" he asked.

The waiter brought the main course—Lobster and Steak—out.

"We worked in reservations for about a year, when we decided to apply to be flight attendants and got hired by Champion Airlines," she said.

"Do you like that better than reservations?" James asked.

"Oh, I love it! We get to travel and get paid for it!" Anna Marie graced him with a smile.

The lobster was scrumptiously bathed in butter, and the steak was so tender it practically melted in their mouths.

They shared laughter over travel adventures. It felt like old times. It felt natural.

James ordered a molten chocolate cake dessert with ice cream for them to share.

After they finished the dessert, James paid the check and they left the restaurant. He drove back to The Royal Islander, where he parked and escorted Anna Marie to the lobby.

"Care to have a drink by the pool?" James smiled at her, hoping for a few more minutes together.

"Okay, just one." She turned and walked out through the sliding glass doors to the pool with James right behind her.

At the bar, she ordered a Baileys on the Rocks, and he ordered a Whiskey on the Rocks. They picked up their drinks and slowly walked toward the large patio overlooking the ocean, where they stopped to gaze out at the clear sky filled with stars. The waves splashed on the shore below them with a rhythm of their own.

At the railing, they sipped their drinks slowly in silence. James set his empty glass down on a table and stood beside Anna Marie, gently placing his arm around her waist.

She finished her drink and set the glass down on the railing. "We positively shouldn't be doing this," Anna Marie said, turning to face James.

"We're both adults and single. Right?" James hesitated for a moment, waiting for her reply.

"Right."

He wasn't about to let this opportunity slip away. Anna Marie welcomed James' lips on hers for a deep kiss filled with all the love and emotions of a more than twenty years wait. Not wanting to overdo it, he ended the kiss, taking her hands in his, moments before Annika, Callie, Yvonne, Thomas, Michael and Samuel stepped onto the patio and walked towards them.

Luckily, Anna Marie had her back to the railing, so hopefully they hadn't all just observed the kiss.

CHAPTER 15

No one said a word about the kiss, so hopefully no one witnessed it.

Annika looped her arm through Anna Marie's and led her toward the pool bar. "Come sit down at the pool bar so I can tell you what we did tonight!"

The whole group walked to the bar and pushed two tables together so they could all sit together.

"So, tell me what you did tonight?" Anna Marie asked.

"We went to Señor Frog's for dinner. All of us went, and it was so much fun!" Annika's eyes were alive with excitement.

"I'm glad you had a good time." Anna Marie smiled.

"Did you have a nice time with James?" Annika probed.

Staring into Annika's happy face, Anna Marie felt a little guilty. Now wasn't the right time, though. "It was a quiet dinner at a place called Fred's. The food was delicious."

"What about James?" Annika whispered in her ear while James got up to talk to the bartender.

"It was okay." Anna Marie unconsciously glanced toward James.

Everyone was laughing and talking while having a good time.

Anna Marie was happy. This was the most fun she'd had in a long time. And the first kiss she'd had in an even longer time. She couldn't help noticing James was smiling at her.

"It's getting late, we should get to bed, we have a big day ahead tomorrow." Yvonne looked toward Anna Marie.

"Yes, we need to get some sleep," Anna Marie replied.

"What are your plans for tomorrow?" Michael asked.

"We're going on a tour to Xel-Ha for the day," Callie answered.

"And the bus picks us up at eight," Anna Marie reminded them.

Everyone stood up and walked to the lobby, where the boys said goodbye to the girls.

James walked up to Anna Marie and asked, "Care to join me for dinner on Friday night?"

"Let me think about it." She turned and walked toward the elevators. The girls and Yvonne followed.

James, Thomas and the boys headed to the parking lot.

The next morning at about ten, they arrived at their destination ready for a day of adventure after an hour and a half bus ride. Xel-Ha was named after a Mayan word meaning 'the place where the waters are born'. An aquatic park that encompassed fourteen acres of jungle and ocean just south of Playa del Carmen.

They swam in serene underground cenotes filled with clear water and caves. Floated down the lazy river in inner tubes. Sat in the sun on the sand of a hidden beach. Did a little snorkeling in the lagoon with tropical fish. Observed the wildlife where the iguanas roamed freely. Their tickets included a buffet, so they dined to their heart's content on Mayan cuisine, seafood and burgers.

"Boy, this day has flown by," Yvonne said as they stood in line to board the tour bus back to the resort.

"I'm exhausted." Annika leaned her head on Anna Marie's shoulder.

"Hey guys, they're boarding. Let's get on." Callie moved quickly to board the bus.

Once seated, the bus began moving and they all fell asleep.

When the bus pulled up to the lobby of The Royal Islander, they woke completely refreshed and ready to enjoy the evening.

"I'm thinking we should shower and change," Yvonne stated. "I definitely need a shower."

"I'm going to take a walk on the beach first and then I'll be up to shower," Annika said.

"Sounds good, I'll join you." Callie ran to catch up with Annika.

"It's just you and me, I guess," Yvonne said.

"They won't be back for a while." A smile crossed Anna Marie's face.

"You thinking what I'm thinking?" Yvonne asked.

"The spa sounds wonderful, let's go!" Anna Marie headed toward the spa.

Minutes later, they were sitting in the sauna, relaxing before slipping into the hot tub.

"This feels so good!" Yvonne exclaimed gleefully.

"Agreed. So glad the spa was included in the all-inclusive." Anna Marie allowed herself to relax. If only the warm water could really soothe away all the stress she felt.

"Now tell me about the kiss." Yvonne giggled.

"What kiss? I have no idea what you're talking about." Anna Marie tried to contain her smile, but soon they were both laughing.

CHAPTER 16

"It was just a kiss." Anna Marie couldn't stop the smile spreading across her face. She couldn't believe it had been almost twenty-four hours since James had kissed her.

"Okay, so was it a friend kiss, a light peck on the lips or a deep passionate kiss?" Yvonne asked with a smirk on her face.

Way too quickly, Anna Marie answered. "Definitely, passionate."

"So, what are you going to do?" Yvonne coyly asked.

"I don't know. I'm still angry that he left and never contacted me again." Memories of that fateful night filled Anna Marie's thoughts.

"Right. And then the whole raising Annika on your own." Yvonne interjected, stating the obvious.

"What do you think I should do?" Anna Marie pondered the pros and cons.

"Well, the question is, who do you tell first?" Yvonne's hands flew up to accentuate her words, splashing water in the air.

"Exactly!" Water dripped from Anna Marie's face, which she quickly wiped away.

Yvonne laughed. "I think it should be James first. That way, you can see how he takes it. He might be furious with you. Realizing that you never tried to find him."

"Really? He has no right to be mad. He was the one who left and never came back." Anna Marie moved to a higher seat to cool down a little bit.

"But didn't you tell him you never wanted to see him again?" Yvonne asked.

"Yes. But that letter was written before I even knew I was pregnant," Anna Marie explained. "Plus, he should've known I was just angry when I wrote it and actually wanted him to come back home to me."

Yvonne moved to a higher seat. "Well, that's most likely what you should tell him so he understands what happened."

"Do you think he will call me at the resort or just show up later tonight?" Anna Marie's mind reeled in anticipation of his next move.

Yvonne was quiet for a moment, then said, "You mean about Friday night? Not sure."

"Yes. He'll want an answer, and I don't have any way to contact him," Anna Marie shrugged.

"We'll figure out a way if he doesn't show up or leave a message," Yvonne said. "Maybe someone at the resort knows him?"

Anna Marie stood up and reached for her towel. "Now that we have that all figured out, we should go back to the room so the girls don't wonder what happened to us."

They rinsed off in the shower, dressed and headed up to their room.

Once in the room, they realized the girls hadn't returned yet.

"I thought for sure they'd be back by now. It's almost eight." Yvonne glanced quickly around the room.

"Maybe they went for a swim in the pool and lost track of time?" Anna Marie asked.

Yvonne walked over to the closet. "Let's get changed and then we can head downstairs to check the pool."

Anna Marie and Yvonne changed into some clean clothes, put on their makeup and went downstairs to look for the girls. They walked out to the pool and only found a family with two small children swimming in the pool.

"What about the pool next door? We can check there." Yvonne headed toward the path that connected the resorts. Anna Marie followed as they both walked at a rapid pace.

Minutes later, they stood, staring at a completely empty pool, with no one in the chairs surrounding it either.

"What do we do now? Is it time to panic?" Anna Marie asked as she quickly scanned their surroundings to see if the girls were anywhere else.

Yvonne glanced at her watch, and it read eight-thirty. It was definitely dark now. They slowly walked back to The Royal Islander, ending up at the front desk.

"I need to talk to James Olson. Do you have any idea how I would go about doing that?" Anna Marie asked.

"Momento, Madam," the clerk walked to the end of the counter. "Enrique, the lady at the counter wants to talk to Mr. Olson. Should we call him?"

"That's the lady he's been spending some time with. Go ahead and call him." The clerk made a call, then walked over to Anna Marie and Yvonne, who were still waiting at the counter. "He'll be here in about ten minutes. So please have a seat."

"Thank you." They complied and sat down on the comfortable, cushiony couch in the lobby to wait.

"I'm really worried that something has happened to them," Anna Marie said.

"Me, too," Yvonne agreed. "They should've been back by now."

Anna Marie stared toward the lobby entrance. "I'm absolutely wishing now that we'd paid the extra cost for the cell service in Mexico."

"Not sure that would've helped. If they actually are in trouble, they presumably wouldn't have an opportunity to use it anyway," Yvonne surmised.

"Oh my God! What if they've been kidnapped?" Anna Marie stood up and began pacing the floor. She almost walked into James as he walked into the lobby through the automatic glass sliding doors. When she saw him, she wrapped her arms around him and began crying.

"What's going on?" He gently tipped her chin up so he could see her face.

"The girls went for a walk on the beach at six-thirty and aren't back yet. We have no idea where they are. What if they've been kidnapped?" Anna Marie's tear-streaked face revealed pure terror.

"Come with me," James said, taking her hand and motioning for Yvonne to follow.

He led them into a large room that appeared to be a sales office. He pointed to a table by the window as he pressed numbers into the phone on the counter. "Send me three security guards."

James joined them at the table and sat down. "Is there anything else you can tell me about the situation?"

"That's all we know," Yvonne replied. "We spent the day at Xel-Ha and returned to the resort at about six-thirty. Annika and Callie decided to go for a walk on the beach, so Anna Marie and I decided to go to the Spa. When we got back, they weren't in the room. We checked the pool here and at The Royal Caribbean next door, and they weren't there. So, we came back here. We had no idea how to contact you, so we asked the front desk. Thank you for coming." Yvonne paced the floor in front of him.

"It's late. It's past eight-thirty. I'm scared," Anna Marie stated. "Where could they be?"

James' answer was another question. "Were Michael and Samuel here?"

"We never saw them," Yvonne stated.

"It's just not like them. They would've known we'd be waiting for them. They would've let us know somehow." Anna Marie stood to look out the glass windows.

"You have to tell him." Yvonne put her arm around Anna Marie's shoulders.

"Tell me what?" James stood in front of her, waiting.

"You should both sit down," Yvonne said and motioned toward the table. To her surprise, they both sat down at the table across from each other.

"Anna Marie, what do you need to tell me?" James' eyes locked on hers.

"I don't know where to start." She felt sheer panic as the fight or flight response options loomed in her mind. Tears began slipping down her cheeks.

"It's always best to start at the beginning." He gently tried to coax her to speak.

"Remember the night before you left?" Anna Marie wiped a tear from her cheek.

"Yes, as if it were yesterday." A hint of regret came through in his voice.

"Well, if you'll recall, we had sex." Anna Marie looked downward, not wanting to meet his gaze.

"Yes." James' voice was soft.

She was barely able to get the words out. "I got pregnant that night."

James's face showed his shock at her statement. "And?"

"I had the baby. Annika." Now she looked directly into his eyes to gauge his reaction.

James stood as he raked his fingers through his hair. "And you couldn't have told me sooner? I have a daughter, and you never told me!" His voice grew louder, but he contained it through his gritted teeth.

"You left! And never came back!" Anna Marie shouted as she stood up and began pacing the floor.

"You said you never wanted to see me again! Remember?" he asked, restating what she'd said in the letter.

"I wrote that letter before I knew I was pregnant. Regardless, you were supposed to have known me well enough to know I didn't mean it." She turned away from him to hide her tears.

"Guys, back to the problem at hand. The girls are missing," Yvonne interrupted.

James walked over to the phone and made another call, this time putting it on speaker so they all could hear.

"Santos. Do you know where Diego and Paulo are? There seems to be two American girls missing from the Islander. I know the boys had them on their radar." James glanced over toward Anna Marie.

"Not sure where the boys are right now, but I can track them down and see if they know anything about these girls. What are their names?" Santos asked.

"Annika and Callie," James replied.

"They must be important for you to call me for a favor?" Santos questioned.

"Annika happens to be my daughter." James glared at Anna Marie.

"What?" Santos' astonished reaction was apparent in his voice.

"It's a long story. I'll tell you later. Let me know if you find out anything." James hung up the phone.

A knock sounded on the door, then three security guards entered the room.

James explained to them that Annika and Callie were missing.

"We're going to search down on the beach. You two can wait here." James briefly glanced toward Yvonne and Anna Marie.

"No! We're coming with you." Anna Marie stopped pacing, directly in front of him.

"You should wait here in case they come back." James offered this more as a command instead of an option.

"We can leave a message at the front desk in case they come back to the resort, but we are coming with you." Anna Marie stood her ground.

"Fine! Have it your way. One question, though, before we go.

Does Annika know?" James had resumed pacing but now stood in front of Anna Marie, searching her eyes for the truth.

"No." Her eyes met his.

"Mighty big secret to keep all these years from the two people you care about most in the world. One that you once loved and one that you love." James exited the room, followed by the security guards.

Anna Marie and Yvonne followed, making sure to stay behind the security guards. For their safety. Once on the beach, the security guards turned on their flashlights and began scanning the beach.

They walked for a few minutes when they heard the muffled screams. "Help! Help us!"

Everyone broke out running down the beach.

CHAPTER 17

Earlier that Evening

Annika and Callie walked down the steps to the beach area, which was filled with chaise lounges lined up in rows, some under umbrellas made of palm branches. They weaved between the chairs until they reached the shore, where the waves came crashing in, walking close enough to get their feet wet.

"It feels so good to walk on this pristine white sand beach and feel the water roll up to our feet," Callie said.

"I know. It's different than the lakes back home. The water is this beautiful turquoise color and so clear."

"Well, that part is like the Minnesota lakes. Crystal clear water."

They continued walking in the same direction they'd taken the day when they'd met Michael and Samuel.

"Do you think we'll accidentally run into them again?" Annika asked.

"Probably not, but it can't hurt to try," Callie said nonchalantly.

"I totally like Michael," Annika paused. "Do you think it's feasible that we could meet up with them back in the States?"

"Definitely! I really like Samuel, and I'm planning to keep in touch with him. I really hope he feels the same."

Walking on the beach requires that you watch where you're walking, so they didn't see Diego and Paulo approaching behind them.

"Hi. What a coincidence to run into you girls here on the beach. How has your vacation been?" Diego asked with his eyes focused on Annika.

They all stopped walking.

"Only one day left, but it's been a lot of fun," Callie answered hesitantly.

"I was hoping we'd see you girls again," Paulo said.

"My dad's house is just up the beach a little way. Care to join us for a drink? You must be thirsty, it's extremely hot out here." Diego turned and walked ahead of them.

They all followed. Annika glanced back to see how far they'd walked away from The Royal Islander to get their bearings.

Diego must've noticed and pointed ahead to a large, white, private residence just a little farther ahead. "Not much further," he smiled.

They kept walking and followed him through a gate where he entered a code before it buzzed and opened. There were stairs on the side of the house, which they followed up to a large veranda and private pool.

"This is beautiful," Callie said.

"Pick a chair and we can relax by the pool." Diego walked over to a cabinet to grab some towels and handed them two each.

"I'll get us some cocktails. Pina Coladas okay with everyone?" Paulo asked.

"Sure," Callie said, and Annika nodded.

Paulo and Diego walked inside the house through a complete wall of sliding glass doors.

"Do you think we should be here?" Annika asked, keeping her voice low.

"I don't know. It feels a bit weird since we don't actually know much about them. At all," Callie said.

"I'm not going into the house. As long as I can see the beach, I think we're okay and can leave when we want to." Annika glanced toward the gate.

"My thoughts exactly. Do you think we'll need a code to open it to leave?" Callie asked.

"Sure, hope not," Annika replied.

Paulo and Diego returned with a tray carrying four Pina Coladas along with a bowl of chips and salsa. They set down the drinks and food on the eight-person table under an upper deck, probably to protect it from the sun and rain.

Annika and Callie got up to take a seat at the table, where Diego handed them each a glass.

The sun was nearing the horizon and would soon be gone, so they'd have to walk back in the dark. Annika had an uneasy feeling in her gut that they were somewhere they shouldn't be. Was the beach safe at night in the dark? She unquestionably wished they'd brought their phones along on their walk. In Mexico, the service was poor and expensive, so they'd opted to use them only in emergencies. Sadly, that didn't do any good if you didn't have the phone with you.

Annika could see that Diego and Paulo were of Spanish blood, and they were blessed with the jet-black hair and chiseled features of the Spaniards. They were striking men, deeply tanned skin, about six feet tall, with rock-hard abs.

"Have you girls had dinner?" Diego asked.

"Cooking is kinda my thing. Fajitas, anyone?" Paulo asked.

Annika looked at Callie, realizing they'd just had a couple of drinks on an empty stomach. At first, she wasn't sure if they should drink the Pina Coladas since she hadn't watched him make them to be sure he hadn't put any drugs into them. You simply never know. He'd let her pick which glass she wanted, and she'd only taken a small sip in the beginning to be certain it was okay. After walking, she was extremely thirsty, so she finally drank it, along with the second one, after watching Diego finish his drink. "Sure, sounds good."

"I'm game," Callie agreed.

They all headed inside the house. Paulo pulled items from the refrigerator, and frying pans were placed on the stove top. He went on to chop up some vegetables, slicing chicken and beef into strips, then tossing them into the already heated pans.

A doorbell rang. Diego excused himself to check on it.

Two guys stepped into the hallway.

Annika saw them looking directly at her and Callie. They seemed eerily the dangerous type.

Diego's deep voice rang out as he spoke rapidly in Spanish, raising his arms to emphasize what seemed to be a stern lecture. The two guys, who appeared to be definitely of the weightlifting, tough-guy types, fired off a rapid reply in Spanish. He then took another lengthy glance toward her and Callie before leaving.

Diego rejoined the group, pulling plates out of a cupboard and setting them on the kitchen table while questioning the girls about what they did back in the States.

"We both recently graduated from college," Callie offered. "How about you guys?"

"Paulo and I attended school at Texas A&M and have degrees in engineering," Diego answered.

"So, you both landed engineering jobs in Cancun?" Annika asked.

"Dinner is served!" Paulo set out the platter of meat and vegetables along with a bowl of beans and a plate of warmed tortilla shells. "Dig in!"

Everyone grabbed a plate and began filling their tortilla shells.

They'd just finished eating when a man walked in through the front door, dressed in a suit. He seemed surprised as he quickly surveyed the room.

"Diego, a moment. In my office." He turned away quickly and walked down the hall.

"Excuse me," Diego said as he stood and followed the man down the hall.

"Who was that?" Callie asked.

"That's his dad." Paulo stared down the hallway.

"Paulo! You too! Down here, now!" the man shouted.

All of a sudden, Annika and Callie were alone in the kitchen.

"I think we need to leave," Annika whispered.

"Yes, this is getting kinda creepy. I think we need to take our chances walking back on the beach." She kept her voice down.

"Not sure what's going on here. Let's go." Annika stood and motioned for Callie to follow her out to the deck, where the steps leading to the gate were located.

They practically ran down the steps, praying the gate wasn't locked from this side. The moment of truth arrived when Annika pressed down on the lever, and it opened. "Thank God!"

They took off running toward the empty beach, as all the tourists were most likely in the resorts, hanging out in their rooms or off to have dinner somewhere. What had they been thinking? They knew better than to have followed Diego and Paulo up to the house. Annika wished they hadn't had that final drink either.

"How far is it to the hotel? I don't remember." Callie stopped dead in her tracks, staring at the two guys blocking their path. She grabbed Annika's hand and moved toward the lower beach closer to the water, but a large, firm hand grabbed her by the arm. The other guy grabbed Callie.

"So, what do we have here?' the larger guy questioned.

"You were at Diego's house, right?" the smaller, built guy asked.

Annika felt positive it was the guys from Diego's house, but why would this guy stop them? What could he possibly want?

"Oh, so you saw us?" the shorter guy said. "Why don't you come with us? We'll show you a good time. Much better than Diego and Paulo can." He pulled Annika against his body and wrapped his fingers in her long hair.

"Let me go!" Annika screamed and pushed against him.

He only tightened his grip and laughed in her face. "Scream all you want, no one will hear you. Or come to help you."

The taller guy reached for Callie and pulled her up against his body as she screamed.

"Help! Someone help us! Please!" Callie yelled and brought her knee up quickly to his groin. He let go, and she ran over to try and help Annika.

Out of the corner of her eye, Callie saw two men running toward them. She had no idea if they were coming to help them escape or to help their attackers. Her freedom was short-lived as the taller guy had regrouped and grabbed her in an iron-tight grip. "Let me go!!"

"Oh, so you thought Diego and Paulo were okay, but not us?" The shorter guy tried to kiss Annika as she swiftly turned her head to the side.

"Release them!" Diego and Paulo shouted as they stopped running a few feet from them.

Annika could see the fear in the shorter guy's eyes. "We were just gonna have a little fun with them, is all."

"Not these two girls. They're American first of all, which will not be good for you. You know that." Diego moved closer.

In the distance, more footsteps could be heard. Oddly, it sounded like they were coming from both directions.

"Diego, help us, please," Annika pleaded, struggling to break free.

The shorter guy eventually let go of Annika when he saw the other people running towards them. He motioned to his friend, who released Callie so abruptly that she fell down on the sand. They ran toward the street, zig-zagging through a resort as fast as they could.

Diego reached out his hand to steady Annika just as Michael came up behind her. Paulo ran to help Callie stand up just as Samuel came running up to them.

"Are you okay?" Michael wrapped Annika in his arms and hugged her tightly to his chest.

"Yes." She sobbed into his shoulder.

"Callie, are you hurt?" Samuel asked as he put his arm around her waist to support her.

"I'm okay," she said and leaned into him.

"Diego, what's going on here?" Michael asked.

"They're fine." Diego glanced behind him quickly.

More movement could be heard on the beach, which meant more people were coming. From both directions.

Diego's dad came into view, flanked by two men carrying guns and large flashlights that were now shining on the group. "Everyone good here?"

"Everything's under control, Dad," Diego said.

Just then, James appeared from the direction of The Royal Islander, accompanied by three security guards with guns.

"Annika. Callie. Are you okay?" James moved closer to look them over to make sure they weren't hurt. After being assured that they were all right, he walked over to Diego. "What the Hell happened here?"

"It wasn't me or Paulo that did anything wrong." Diego was the first to answer.

"No? So those two thugs weren't doing your dirty work?" James asked.

"Definitely not! And I had no idea she was your daughter, Mr. Olson. If I'd known, I wouldn't have gone anywhere near her or her friend." Diego stood defiantly in front of James.

Anna Marie and Yvonne arrived at the scene, making their way through the crowd to reach their girls. Each one immediately hugged their daughter.

Annika broke the embrace and backed away a bit. "What did you just say?" She walked over to Diego while everyone watched.

"I'm sorry, I didn't know Mr. Olson was your dad," Diego stated.

"And who is Mr. Olson?" Annika asked.

"James Olson," Diego stated matter-of-factly.

He said it in a way that made her think this was something everyone else knew. Except her!

"Mom! What is going on here? That can't possibly be true, right? My dad is dead."

"Annika, I'm so sorry. I didn't want you to find out this way," Anna Marie pleaded.

Callie attempted to comfort her, but Annika pushed her arm back, turned away from them all, and slowly walked back to the resort alone.

Minutes later, Callie ran to catch up with her.

James nodded to one of the security guards, and he followed them, staying a few steps behind.

"We done here?" Santos asked James.

"Yes."

With that, Santos, his men, Diego, and Paulo turned around and began walking back to their house.

"Anna Marie, I'm sorry," James said, moving to stand in front of her.

She stared into his eyes, unable to hold back the tears. "I have to go." She turned, but not before tears flooded her eyes, heading slowly back to the resort.

Yvonne quickly ran to catch up with her.

Another security guard fell in step behind them.

James waved toward Michael and Samuel to follow them. They nodded and walked a few steps behind the guards.

The last security guard followed behind Michael and Samuel.

James had been left standing on the beach in the sand as the waves slowly rolled toward the shore in the moonlight. Alone.

CHAPTER 18

Annika and Callie were the first to arrive back at The Royal Islander, followed of course by the security guard.

"Annika, are you okay?" Callie asked as they sat down on a couch in the lobby.

"No." She didn't have any idea what to do, so she just sat quietly with her head in her hands.

A few minutes later, Yvonne and Anna Marie walked into the lobby, followed by another security guard.

Callie wrapped her arm around Annika's shoulder. This is how Anna Marie and Yvonne found them.

"We need to talk," Anna Marie said to Annika as she tried to touch her shoulder, but her hand was pushed away.

Annika looked up. "My-whole-life-I-thought-he-was-dead."

"I'm sorry. Can we talk about it? Please let me explain," Anna Marie pleaded.

"I can't right now. Callie and I are going to stay in the lock-off room. Maybe tomorrow." Annika stood and walked toward the elevator with Callie.

Anna Marie watched the elevator door open and close, just like the door to her heart.

After the door closed, Michael and Samuel walked into the lobby through the automatic-opening glass doors.

Michael looked around the room for Annika and Callie. "Aren't the girls here?"

"They just left to go to their room. They don't want to talk about it right now," Yvonne offered.

"Oh...we'll just stop by tomorrow," Michael said as he and Samuel tipped their heads to the ladies. They walked out of the resort's doors leading to the street.

The security guards stood by the lobby door leading to the pool.

Anna Marie sat down in a chair that looked out over the pool area, and Yvonne pulled a chair over to sit beside her. They both watched as James walked through the glass doors with the last security guard. He walked over to where the ladies were seated.

Anna Marie hesitantly raised her head and looked up at him.

His tense body hovered above her. "I'm going home. Tomorrow, we need to have a conversation. Just you and me. And after we're done, I want to talk to Annika. I'll leave a message for you with the front desk tomorrow morning." James walked out through the lobby doors to the waiting bellman.

"Well, guess we're the last man standing, as they say. We should probably head up to the room," Yvonne coaxed.

"She hates me. He hates me. My life is over," Anna Marie said and burst into tears.

Yvonne pulled her to a standing position, and they made their way over to the elevator. It would be a long night for everyone. She put Anna Marie to bed. An hour later, the crying finally stopped, which hopefully meant she'd fallen asleep. Lying down on the other side of the king-sized bed, Yvonne eventually allowed her eyes to close.

∽

"I need a taxi," James said.

"Yes, sir." The bellman called a taxi.

James found Michael and Samuel waiting at his house.

"I thought I told you to keep Diego and Paulo away from the girls?" He tossed his keys into a dish on an entry table, then sat down in his favorite leather chair.

"How were we supposed to think they would take off down the beach in the dark?" Michael asked.

Samuel added, "Especially, after a full day at Xel-Ha?"

"So, what happened on the beach?" James asked.

"We talked to Diego," Michael conveyed. The girls were walking down the beach. He invited them to have a drink at his dad's house, then made some food."

"That's when a couple of his guys showed up. They made some snide remarks about the girls before leaving," Samuel added as he paced in front of James' chair.

James listened intently. "Continue."

"Apparently, that's about the time you called Santos. He must've immediately driven home. When he got there, he called Diego into his office and minutes later called Paulo into the office, too."

"So, he saw the girls right when he walked in?" James asked.

"He was angry when he saw them." Michael paced the floor and paused. "The girls left while they were in the office."

"When Santos finished yelling at them," Samuel explained. They walked back to the kitchen and realized the girls were gone. The gate wasn't closed properly, so they assumed they'd left to go back via the beach and went to find them."

"And?" James grew impatient.

"Diego realized that his guys hadn't left but instead were waiting on the beach for the girls. They followed them and confronted them."

"Did they touch the girls?" James was furious. He slammed a fist into the arm of his chair and stood. "This is why I told you to watch them!"

"You never told us Annika was your daughter," Michael stated as calmly as he could.

"You didn't answer my question!" James shouted.

"Diego wasn't sure. The guys ran off when they saw him and Paulo approaching. He doesn't think they would've had any time to..." Samuel paused.

"Damn it!" James yelled. "I guess I'll just have to ask Annika myself tomorrow."

"Why didn't you tell us you were her dad?" Michael asked again.

"Because I didn't know. Anna Marie told me right after she told me Annika and Callie were missing," James walked over to the bar and poured himself a whiskey straight up, downed it in one swallow, and walked out onto his deck overlooking the ocean. "You can see yourselves out."

James heard the door shut and knew they were gone.

What the hell happened tonight? His life had been turned completely upside down in a matter of hours. His first love shows up at his resort, whom he hasn't seen in over twenty years, and then tells him he has a daughter. That was a lot without the whole part of her being missing.

He needed to process the situation and have his head on straight because tomorrow he was going to meet his daughter. They definitely had a lot of catching up to do. He wasn't sure what to say to her, but he knew there wasn't anything more he wanted to do than be a part of her life from now on.

Anna Marie, however, was another whole matter. He knew he'd never stopped loving her. A guy never forgets his first love. He just wasn't sure he could forgive her for not trying to contact him all these years. But then he'd never tried to connect with her all these years either. Maybe the person he should be mad at was himself!

CHAPTER 19

ANNIKA COULDN'T SLEEP. SNAPSHOTS OF JAMES WHIRLED through her head. Almost like a movie filled with every interaction she'd had with him the past few days. She tried to turn off the movie screen in her head, but she couldn't stop thinking about James. James Olson. He was her dad? Her whole life, she believed the reason she didn't have a dad was because he died in Vietnam. Why hadn't her mom told her the truth? That was the big question. She was so uncontrollably angry with her mom that she didn't dare talk to her yet. It had always been just her and her mother, and they were so close. She simply didn't understand why she'd lied. Wanting to give her mom the benefit of the doubt, she sincerely hoped there had been a good reason.

A really good reason!

The clock on the nightstand read three o'clock. In the morning. Callie was sound asleep on the other bed, and she should be sleeping too. Would counting sheep work? She'd never tried it. Somewhere she'd heard just counting backwards from 100 worked. The sheep seemed weird, so she opted to count backwards. She desperately needed to put a different perspective on the whole *James* situation.

Sleep was needed, but she still couldn't seem to shut down her mind, so she could drift off to never-never land.

Well, I'll give it a try. 100, 99, 98...

Annika slowly opened her eyes to see the bright sun shining in through the slight crack in the heavy blackout curtains. She glanced over to the other bed and saw it was empty, meaning Callie was already up. The clock on the nightstand read nine-thirty. Her stomach rumbled, and she made her way to the bathroom. The door to the adjoining room was closed. Good. She wasn't ready to see anyone yet anyway. Maybe after a shower.

On the other side of the door, in the living room area, Yvonne and Callie heard the shower turn on.

"Well, looks like Annika is up," Callie said.

"Anna Marie's shower turned on a little bit ago," Yvonne stated. "Not sure what's going to happen when they're done, but they need to talk it out."

"Maybe we should leave them alone, go down and take a walk on the beach, then have breakfast?" Callie questioned.

"Sounds like a good plan." Yvonne stood, picked up her beach bag and key card, as Callie did the same. They left the room, leaving mother and daughter to sort it out on their own.

After her shower, Anna Marie made her way to the kitchen to make a cup of coffee. Caffeine was definitely needed to start this day. Wrapped in her robe, coffee cup in hand, she headed through the sliding glass door to the large patio of their penthouse villa and sat down at the table. Gazing out toward the turquoise ocean water rolling to shore, she wondered how she'd gotten to this point.

Everyone was mad as hell at her. Well, not everyone, but the person she loved more than anyone didn't want to talk to her.

She hadn't meant to devastate Annika, she truthfully hadn't even thought about James all these years because in her mind, he was dead. That had been the only way she'd made it through the past years. Knowing now that he was still alive but never came looking for her, hurt so incredibly much and still caused unbelievable pain. She quickly wiped a tear that had managed to slide down her cheek. He definitely hadn't loved her! That had been the only reason he would've moved on and never looked back. In the midst of way too many years of heartbreak caused by his shocking departure, she'd hurt Annika now, too.

Annika walked out of her bedroom and saw her mother sitting at the patio table. She tightened her robe, inhaled deeply, took a deep breath and joined her mother. "One question. Why?"

Anna Marie turned from staring at the bright sun shining on the absolutely gorgeous, shimmering ocean to face her daughter, with red, swollen eyes from crying herself to sleep last night. She raked her fingers through her freshly washed hair. "Baby, I'm so sorry."

"Mom, sorry, just isn't going to cut it right now. I need to know why I never knew James Olson was my dad." Annika locked gazes with her mom's eyes.

"I don't even know where to start." Anna Marie turned her chair.

"The beginning is perhaps the best place." Annika continued staring at her mom.

"Okay. We were high school sweethearts, which you already knew."

"Well, at least that part is true then." Annika didn't try to disguise the disdain in her voice.

"Yes. I assumed we would get married after graduation. Had already begun planning the wedding in my head." Anna Marie shifted nervously in her chair.

"Did he know this?" Annika asked.

"I guess, to be honest, I talked about it and he said there was no rush. We were planning on going off to college, so I assumed he most likely wanted to wait until after we graduated. I thought at least we could get engaged." Anna Marie glanced back toward the ocean.

"So did he propose?"

"No." Flashbacks from high school raced through her head. "This is hard. It's extremely personal. And private."

"What? I think we're past that point. Go on."

"We were so young. Just barely 18. We were in love."

"And..."

"It was different back then. The possibility of getting pregnant was a huge concern. This was just the beginning of birth control pills. They were scary, no one knew much about them or the possible side effects. *Blood clots.* A girl I knew back then went on the pill, got a blood clot, causing her to lose her peripheral vision, and was in the hospital for days. They were much stronger, with higher dosages, because they didn't have much history with them yet. Plus, they weren't as easy to get as they are now."

"What are you saying?" Annika leaned forward in her chair, resting her elbows on the table.

"I was terrified of getting pregnant. I didn't want to go on the pill because I was afraid of it. So, we simply didn't have sex." Anna Marie searched Annika's face. This was so hard.

"OMG! You must've, or I wouldn't be here right now!" Annika raised her voice.

"Only once. Who gets pregnant the first time? It was the end of the summer, college would be starting in a week, and James still hadn't decided where he was going. His parents were Up North in cabin country, so we had the house to ourselves. Things got carried away. He used a condom." Anna Marie shifted her gaze back to Annika, searching for her understanding.

"Well, obviously it was defective." Annika sighed and leaned back in her chair.

Anna Marie gazed out toward the ocean, deep in thought, before answering. "The next day, he informed me he'd joined the Army and would be gone for four years. He thought it would be best if we were able to see other people because he wasn't sure he'd be coming back home to Minneapolis."

Sympathy washed over Annika's face. "So, what did you do?"

"Cried a lot. After a few weeks, when I still hadn't heard anything from him, I sent him a letter saying I never wanted to see him again. I was so inevitably angry," Anna Marie admitted.

"Cell phones and computers weren't apparently a thing back then. From what you've said, I totally get it." Annika reached over to hold Anna Marie's hand.

"I thought he'd know that I still loved him and didn't mean what I'd said in the letter, but I never heard from him again." A wave of relief rolled through Anna Marie.

"So, he never knew?"

"I'd started college but had to drop out. I realized I was pregnant right away when I missed my period a few weeks later. I somehow managed to finish the first semester even though I felt miserable and nauseated all the time." Tears rolled down Anna Marie's cheeks.

Annika moved her chair next to her mom and slid her arm around her shoulders. "And your heart was broken in a million pieces."

Anna Marie nodded her head. "Thankfully, my mother and father were there for me, or I never would've made it through. They helped me so much. Let me live with them and supported me in keeping the baby. You."

"Thank you, Mom." Now Annika was crying, too.

"I guess I was ashamed of having sex and not being married for a long time. It was still so taboo back then. When you started asking about where your dad was, how could I explain this to a small child? It was easiest to say he was gone, which he was. For the longest time, you never questioned it. But when you got older and he'd still never contacted me, I decided it would be best if you thought he'd died in the military, since he'd joined the Army." Anna Marie's relief was apparent.

"But you never thought to tell me the truth once I was older?" Annika asked.

"Like you said, there wasn't the internet back then, so there wasn't any way to try and locate him. And why would I have wanted to anyway? To me, he was dead. Even if I didn't have any proof. It was easier that way." Anna Marie hesitated before answering. "I think I'd convinced myself that he actually was dead, so I could move on. That way, I didn't have to think about the fact that he simply didn't love me or want me enough to come back home after his four years of enlistment."

"We have internet now," Annika stated what she knew was obvious.

"I know." Anna Marie rubbed her hands together as nerves got the best of her. "It got to the point that I didn't want to know what ultimately happened to him. We'd managed just fine without him. And I didn't want to have my heart broken into a million pieces again."

"Now that we know he is alive and right here in Cancun, what do we do?" Annika asked.

"It's definitely time for the three of us to talk." Anna Marie had ultimately come to terms with the fact that the secret, which had been such a big part of her life, was no longer a secret. It felt as if a huge rock had been lifted off her chest. She could finally breathe again. She'd hidden this story for way too long.

"Yes," Annika agreed.

"Do you want me to contact him? Or do you want to?" Anna Marie asked.

Annika placed her hand on her mother's. "Probably should be you, Mom."

"Breakfast first?" Anna Marie asked.

Annika jumped up out of her chair. "Makeup and clothes first! Then breakfast!"

CHAPTER 20

THE ROYAL ISLANDER'S FRONT DESK HAD BEEN INFORMED TO have a message left on Anna Marie's room phone to come to the front desk to pick up an envelope that had been left for her. He'd thought about what his next move should be practically the whole night. His adrenaline was running high after little sleep and three cups of black coffee. At seven, when he finally gave up on sleeping, he sat at his desk writing a short note to Anna Marie.

I'd like to invite you and Annika to lunch at my home. I'll have a car sent to pick you up at noon. The three of us have a lot to talk about.

James

He sealed the envelope and had his assistant deliver it to the resort.

Now all he had to do was wait and think about what he would say to Anna Marie and Annika. And hopefully, figure out how to turn this life-changing situation into a happy life going forward, for all of them. He'd missed so much. They'd missed so much. Luckily, they all still had many years ahead of them and hopefully could spend them together. His heart was filled with so much love that had just been waiting for the right people to share it with, and now he'd found them.

He walked into the kitchen where Maria, his cook, was busy preparing lunch.

"Don't worry, I have everything under control for your special guests," Maria assured him.

James knew from the look on Maria's face that she knew who his 'special guests' were. He shook his head and smiled. "It seems there are no secrets in this house."

"I'm going to do everything I can to make them feel welcome in your home." Maria smiled. "Don't worry."

"Like that's even an option." James walked out to the deck.

He saw Michael and Samuel standing out on the deck of Thomas' house. Presumably waiting to see if the girls showed up walking down the beach or at his house. After relaxing in his favorite chair and listening to the rhythmic sound of the waves rolling to shore for over an hour, he got up to take a shower.

After dressing, Anna Marie and Annika were heading out the door when they noticed a light blinking on the room's phone. Annika picked up the receiver, pressed a button to listen to the message, then hung up. "There's an envelope at the front desk for you to pick up, Mom."

"Okay, we can get it on our way to breakfast." Anna Marie closed the door behind them, and they walked to the elevator.

"Hi, I received a message to pick up an envelope here," Anna Marie stated as she stepped up to the counter.

"Your name?" the clerk asked.

"Anna Marie Johnson."

The reception clerk nodded and reached behind him for the envelope sitting on the shelf behind him. He placed it on the counter in front of her.

"Thank you," Anna Marie said as she picked it up and turned away.

"Aren't you going to open it?" Annika asked.

Anna Marie kept walking. "Once we get a table and are seated."

"Who do you think it's from?" Annika stared at the envelope.

"I'm guessing it's from James." Anna Marie held it up to glance at the handwriting.

Once seated at a table outside on the restaurant's patio overlooking the pool, Anna Marie set the letter on the table. From what she could remember, it looked like his handwriting. She could feel Annika's eyes watching her, so she carefully opened it and took out the letter. She read it quickly, then laid it on the table so Annika could see it.

Anna Marie,

I'd like to invite you and Annika to lunch at my home. I'll have a car sent to pick you up at noon. The three of us have a lot to talk about.

James

"I want to go," Annika said.

"Okay, I think we should too." Anna Marie nodded in agreement.

The waiter brought them glasses filled with orange juice and water. Then they headed up to the breakfast buffet.

When they got back to their table, they found Yvonne and Callie had just been seated at the table next to them. They all laughed. Then Yvonne and Callie joined Anna Marie and Annika at their table.

"So, everyone happy this morning?" Yvonne asked.

"Getting there," Annika said.

"Well, we know food always helps," Callie offered.

The waiter noticed they'd moved tables and dropped off their drinks at the new table.

"I'm getting food." Callie headed up to the buffet with her mom right behind her.

Soon, they were all happily sampling all the delectable items from the buffet.

"Any word from James?" Yvonne asked.

"He invited us to lunch at his house. He's sending a car to pick us up at noon," Annika stated.

"Oh, well that's good news, isn't it?" Yvonne asked.

"We do need to talk, so I guess this will work," Anna Marie answered.

"Glad to see a little smile on your face," Yvonne said.

"I want to give him a chance to tell his side of the story," Annika added.

Anna Marie hoped this meeting went well. It was, realistically, partly her fault for not searching him out. But only a small part. She'd had a light breakfast, knowing they'd be eating again soon. Annika, on the other hand, could eat a whole meal and still be hungry. Luckily, she'd been blessed with a great metabolism.

When they were done eating, they headed back up to the room so Anna Marie could change. She wanted to look her best for their meeting with James.

CHAPTER 21

A LITTLE BEFORE NOON, ANNA MARIE AND ANNIKA WALKED outside the lobby doors and saw what they assumed was James' Suburban waiting for them.

The driver walked up to them. "Anna Marie Johnson?"

"Yes." Anna Marie stared at the midnight black Suburban. Would it be taking her to more heartbreak?

The driver opened the back seat doors and motioned for them to get in.

"Mom? Are you okay?" Annika asked.

Anna Marie's stomach was churning in anticipation of talking to James, and she felt her anxiety rising. There was no question in her mind that this needed to be done, though, so she nodded and stepped into the Suburban. After the door closed and the vehicle made its way down Kukulcan Boulevard, she felt her chest tighten, and it became harder to breathe. She began taking deep breaths of air and exhaling slowly.

Annika reached over to hold her hand. "It'll be okay. I love you, Mom. Nothing is going to change that."

"I'll be okay. It's just an anxiety attack." She continued doing the deep breathing technique she'd learned years ago to get through it.

"I know. Just relax. Remember, we're doing this together," Annika stated.

Anna Marie leaned back on the seat and closed her eyes while she continued to take deep breaths. She tried to focus on all the good things in her life. A job she loved. A daughter whom she loved and was forever thankful for. It seemed like only a few minutes and only a few blocks had gone by when they turned into a private driveway and the Suburban stopped.

The driver exited the vehicle and opened the door for them. He motioned to the pathway leading to the door, rang the bell, then turned and walked back towards the Suburban.

Anna Marie wasn't sure she could make it through the meeting at this point. Her body jerked involuntarily when the door opened. It wasn't James.

"Welcome! You must be Anna Marie and Annika. So happy to meet you. I'm Maria, James' cook." She motioned for them to come in and led them up a small staircase to a massive room overlooking the ocean. "Please have a seat. James will be right with you. I've prepared a special lunch for you. Please make yourselves comfortable. I'll let you know when lunch is served." She left the room.

Neither Anna Marie nor Annika had said a word, as Maria had not stopped talking since opening the door.

"Mom, can you believe this view?" Annika walked over to look out the wall-to-wall glass windows with sliding glass doors in the center leading to a huge covered patio facing the ocean.

Anna Marie managed to sit down on a super comfy-looking couch. She'd been so strong all these years. What was wrong with her? The anxiety attacks had been few and far between, and she'd learned to cope with them. But now that she thought about it, this was the perfect setting for one.

"Ladies, welcome to my home. So happy you are here," James said as he walked into the large room. He walked over to the window where Annika was still standing. "Always is a spectacular view." He turned back to Anna Marie. "Thanks for coming."

"There literally wasn't a choice," she managed to get out.

"Are you feeling all right? You look a bit pale." He sat down next to her and picked up her cold hand.

"Oh, it's nothing really. Meeting you triggered a panic attack, that's all." Anna Marie shifted slightly to sit up, as she'd been slouched back on the cushions, removing her hand from his.

"Is there anything I can do to help you?" he asked.

"Massaging her shoulders usually helps," Annika offered.

Anna Marie gave her a 'I can't believe you just said that' look.

"Turn a little and let me help you through this." James began massaging her shoulders.

Anna Marie leaned into his massage and turned her head to the side to release some of the tension in her neck. "I don't want to do this." Tears were welling in her eyes, then rolling down her cheeks.

Annika watched from where she was still standing by the windows. She was concerned for her mom.

James tenderly turned Anna Marie toward him, putting his arms around her.

"There's going to be a whole lot of adjusting on everyone's part, but hopefully it will be good for all of us." He gently massaged Anna Marie's back while he held her.

"Maybe, I could've prevented this whole mess if I'd tried to contact you years ago," Anna Marie stated.

Annika walked over and sat in the chair beside the couch. "It's not your fault, Mom."

"Is that what you think?" James released Anna Marie so he could look her in the eyes. "That it's your fault?"

"Yes."

"If this is anyone's fault, it's mine. I take the full blame," James stated.

"Maybe we should discuss this between the three of us, starting at the beginning. I'd like to hear both of your recollections about what happened." Annika faced her parents. "Okay?"

"Yes. Who do you want to go first?" James asked.

Annika looked into her father's blue eyes. "I'd like to hear your version of the story first."

"Okay. Some of this you will undoubtedly already know since it will be the same as your mother's." He stood to pace the floor. "I met Anna Marie in high school. We dated the entire time, and we were in love. The summer after graduation was great. We spent it going to the lake and hanging out with our friends. A few of them had gotten engaged, and I knew she expected that we would, too. Since I was a little boy, I wanted to fly airplanes. Back then, the only way to get the training and experience was to join the military."

"I loved you, Anna Marie." He paused to look into her eyes. "I almost gave up my dream of becoming a pilot and went to college. You'd been accepted to a couple of schools, and I knew that's what you wanted to do. At the end of the summer, I knew I'd always regret it if I didn't pursue my dream, so I joined the Army. Vietnam was rough, and a lot of guys didn't make it back. I thought I was doing you a favor by breaking up with you. That way, you could go to college, and if you met someone else, you could pursue it without worrying about whether I was going to make it back. I think in the back of my mind, I thought I would come back after my enlistment was done, and if you were still single, maybe you'd take me back."

"I think you're leaving out an important part of this situation. Me." Annika's eyes misted over.

"Yes. A huge mistake on my part." James watched the tears break free and roll down her cheeks.

"Who, me?" Annika asked.

"No, not you. That's not what I meant. You could never be a mistake." James flashed her a big smile. "I meant I need to discuss that part also. I'm sorry, I'm not very good at this."

"Continue, James," Anna Marie coaxed.

"I loved you, Anna Marie, so much. That night at my parents' house, we got carried away. And that time we didn't stop. Because you were afraid of taking the pill, we'd done everything but have intercourse for the past three years. I'd gotten a condom from a friend just in case we changed our minds and I decided to stay and attend college. Because if I stayed, I was going to propose. Even had a ring."

"I never knew that," Anna Marie said.

"I was young and selfish. I wanted you to be able to go to college, I wanted to fly planes, but I'd loved you all through high school, and I didn't want to miss out on the culmination of that love." James paused. "Ultimately, I used the condom, and when I was taking it off in the bathroom afterwards, I noticed it was leaking. I thought it was okay, because no one gets pregnant from doing it once. Right?"

"Obviously, that's only a myth." Anna Marie sighed deeply.

"Proof is right here," Annika said.

"I left for boot camp the next morning. I figured you hated me, but I wanted you to make something of your life and not sit around waiting for someone who might not make it back. My father took a job in Denver a few months after I left, and they moved immediately. I went to see them once after about two years. Mom had boxed all my stuff up when they'd moved. The boxes were all sitting in a bedroom. I didn't know where I was going to end up, so I just left them there unopened."

"Are my grandparents still alive?" Annika asked.

"Yes," James answered.

"Continue," Anna Marie coaxed.

"When my enlistment time of four years was up, I had enough flying hours in to apply to the airlines. I went to Denver, where my parents were living and started applying with all the major airlines. I stayed with them until I landed a job with Continental Airlines. Once I got my own place, an apartment near the airport, I finally opened the boxes and found your letter, Anna Marie." His eyes scoured her beautiful face for forgiveness. "It was over four years after you'd written it. I could feel your pain and the anger in your words. It'd been so long that I assumed at that point that you'd most likely moved on and were possibly married to someone else by that time. It broke my heart to know how horribly I'd broken yours."

"I never meant a word of it, you know. I still loved you." Anna Marie got up and walked over to the window.

"Go on," Annika insisted.

"I started with commuter planes and worked my way up to the big planes, Boeing 747s. When I had enough seniority, I opted to fly international routes. Those gave you a lot of free time since I basically only had to work about one week a month. I still have a home in Denver." James glanced out the window toward the ocean.

"So how did you end up in Cancun?" Annika asked.

"There are four of us who were in the Army together, and then after we were discharged, we all landed jobs with Continental Airlines. We opted for a lot of the Caribbean International routes. On my first trip to Cancun, I couldn't get over how beautiful it was. I loved the sun, the warm temps, and the beautiful white-sand beaches with crystal-clear turquoise water. Back then, there wasn't anything here. Only miles and miles of empty coastline. The land was cheap, so we each bought enough to build a house, and then we decided to buy more land to build timeshares. We wanted others in the US to have the opportunity to enjoy what we were able to enjoy all the time. First, we built one past the downtown area called The Royal Cancun. Once that property was sold, we purchased a large coastal tract to build three more resorts. We built them one at a time. First, The Royal Mayan, next The Royal Caribbean and lastly The Royal Islander."

"So, you own all four resorts?" Annika asked in shock.

"Our company, The Royal Resorts, manages the properties until their thirty-year leases are up. We make money as the managing company, but we also made money up front on each property after they were built."

Anna Marie started crying again, but tried to hide it. She could tell he had no idea why.

"Anna Marie?" he asked.

"Do you have any idea how hard it was to raise a child alone? Money was difficult, and there was very little." Anna Marie sat back down on the couch. He had no idea what she'd been through.

"Mom, your turn. I know you told me a little bit this morning, but I want to hear the whole story," Annika coaxed.

Anna Marie wiped at her tear-stained cheek with a Kleenex she pulled out of her purse. Then blew her nose before beginning. "As you already know, James and I dated all through high school. We were in love, and I thought we'd get engaged and then be off to college together, getting married after we got our degrees. At the end of the summer, I was totally blindsided when James broke up with me after a wonderful night of making love. It was my first time. The next day after he left, I wasn't even able to comprehend what had just happened to us. For days, I kept thinking he'd change his mind and come back. Or at least call me. I was willing to wait for him if his dream to fly planes included the Army. But the days silently slipped by with no contact from him. Each day, I got angrier with him, feeling like I'd just wasted three years loving someone who didn't want me anymore. These feelings prompted the letter."

"Which I didn't get for over four years," James stated as he shook his head.

"I didn't know that." Anna Marie hesitated for a moment before continuing. "Then I missed my period. At first, I thought it was just going to be an off month because I was so upset, but then the nausea set in, and I missed the next one. There was no doubt I was pregnant."

"I'm so sorry I wasn't there to help you," James said.

"It was a totally different time back then. I had to tell my parents. I had no idea if they would be on board with me keeping the baby, because not keeping it wasn't even an option in my mind. They'd warned me not to have sex, because I might get pregnant. For the best part, we listened and did everything we could not to risk taking that chance. They could've kicked me out when I told them, but I think they were suffering the loss of you, James, too. You'd become a part of my family's lives, too, after our three years of dating. But they were saints and welcomed their new grandchild into their home with open arms."

"They were and are the most loving grandparents any child could ask for. They've always been there for me," Annika added.

"If it hadn't been for them, I never would have been able to finish college. They allowed us to live with them and took care of Annika while I was in class. It wasn't until after Travel School and I landed my first job at MLT Vacations that I was able to rent an apartment for Annika and me. Once I transitioned into a flight attendant, I was finally able to buy a house. Definitely nothing like this." The tears threatened again.

"It's okay, Mom. You and I had a great life together. We were able to travel around the world. We didn't have all the luxuries of fancy hotels or food, but we got to experience the history of other countries and other states. I love you, and I love the life we've had so far." Annika hugged her mother.

"I am so sorry." He paused for a moment as a troubled look crossed his face. "If I could go back in time, I would've proposed. I've missed so much."

"That's not a possibility," Anna Marie said. "It's over and done with."

"Where did you tell Annika that her father was?" James asked.

"What was I supposed to say?" she asked defiantly.

James was silent.

"She was a baby. Should I have told her that her dad left after we had sex and never returned?" Anna Marie asked.

"Probably not," he agreed.

"When she was little, she would ask. I didn't know what to say to a child, so I decided to tell her you were in the military and died. In my eyes, you were dead, so that story worked." Anna Marie ran her fingers through her hair. "When she got older and would bring it up, I decided that since I'd never heard from you again, I would simply stick to that story. Eventually, she stopped asking."

"Did you try to find me?" he asked.

"Why?" Anna Marie locked eyes with him. "You obviously hadn't contacted me, so that meant you didn't want to see me. Or our daughter."

"If I'd known..." James hesitated.

"You'd have come back for her? But not for me?" Anna Marie began sobbing at this point.

"That's not what I meant. If I'd even thought you'd want to see me again, I would've contacted you. But after reading that letter, all my hopes of making amends were shattered." James sat down on the couch, took Anna Marie in his arms and began stroking her hair, as she sobbed against his chest. "I'm sorry for all the pain I've caused you. I never stopped loving you."

Annika sat on the other side of Anna Marie and wrapped her arms around her mother, also.

CHAPTER 22

Maria was listening to the conversation from down the hallway. Tears slipped down her cheeks. She loved James like a son after working for him all these years. She'd been keeping the lunch warm all this time. It was time to serve it.

She walked into the room. "Lunch is served."

James looked up and nodded her way. "Let's go eat," he said. "Maria has prepared a special lunch for you." He stood, took Anna Marie's hand to help her up, and gently placed his hand on her back to guide her to the patio, where lunch was waiting for them. Annika followed her parents.

As soon as they were seated, Maria brought out her famous Mexican Street Tacos on a brightly colored, red-and-yellow ceramic platter. Their glasses were perfectly placed on the table, filled with iced margaritas. The rims were even dusted in crystallized sugar. Another bowl sat on the table, full of freshly made corn chips and smaller bowls of homemade salsa and fresh avocado guacamole. A large, clear vase rested in the center of the table, filled with a fresh floral masterpiece: bird of paradise, Mexican marigolds, Laelia orchids, roses, and dahlias.

Unfortunately, they all sat in silence at the table.

Unexpectedly, Maria clapped her hands. "Everyone, please eat!"

The sudden clapping noise snapped them out of their trance-like state. Annika picked up the platter, placed two tacos on her plate, then passed it to her mother. Soon, all their plates were filled, and they began enjoying their lunch.

After tasting her first bite, Annika remarked, "This is delicious. Maria is a great cook."

"Yes, she is. Hired her over fifteen years ago after tasting these tacos. Best cook in Cancun." James nodded in Maria's direction.

"So do you spend most of your time in Cancun or Denver?" Annika asked.

"Possibly a bit more in Denver, to be honest. It gets extremely hot here in the summer, so I head to Denver." James beamed toward his daughter. "But I also like skiing in the winter, so I spend some time during the winter in Breckenridge. The rest of the winter, I'm down here."

"I love skiing, too. Mom and I try to head to Denver at least once every winter for a ski weekend." Annika smiled at her mother. "She enjoyed skiing so much, she made sure I learned to ski at Buck Hill in Burnsville."

"Anna Marie and I learned to ski at Hyland Hills in Blooming-ton, our sophomore year." He glanced toward Anna Marie. "She was always a better skier than I was."

"I don't know about that. From what I remember, you were certainly good, and that's why you joined the High School ski team," Anna Marie stated.

"You were asked to join, too." James' voice filled with pride.

"I had no idea, Mom," Annika said.

"I like skiing and am a pretty decent skier. I basically didn't love skiing in Minnesota enough to want to be out there skiing every day in freezing temps," Anna Marie admitted.

"Well, I'd love to have you both come to Denver for a ski week and stay with me this year. Once the snow starts falling, you can send me some dates that work for you, and I'll try to adjust my schedule to make it work," James offered.

"I'd love that! Mom?" Annika asked.

"You can certainly go if you want to." Anna Marie looked at James. "It's your choice. I'm going to have to think about it. Not sure if it would be a good choice for me."

"No strings attached. Just a fun week skiing." James posed a very sincere look on his face for her.

Anna Marie couldn't help chuckling a bit. He was the same old James. The one she loved and the one she despised. Yes, that was a good choice of words. Hate was a strong word, and she knew she didn't hate him. She was merely angry at him and the world for what had kept them apart all these years. Was it all his fault? Not in reality. She should've tried harder to find him and talk to him, too. He should've come back to say he was sorry, so they could've made up and been one happy family. But that hadn't happened. Now so many years had gone by. Was it even possible to reignite their love for each other? He'd said he was sorry and had never stopped loving her. Was that enough to at least give it a try?

"Maybe. That's all you get right now. Okay?" Anna Marie gave him a little smile.

"I'd like to get to know you better. I've never had a dad, so I'm not sure how all of this works, but I'm game to spend a week skiing in Denver. I'll have to see if I can get time off. But first I have to find a job!" Annika laughed.

Soon, James and Anna Marie joined in, and they were all laughing.

"Okay, we have a plan then. Two possible yeses. I can work with that!" James said.

Their spirits had been lifted by telling their stories of the years that had passed, while realizing each of them had reasons for their past decisions in life. Now, hopefully, they could all move forward together.

Maria walked in carrying a Chocolate Layer Cake on a large pedestal cake plate, a knife and a serving spatula.

"That looks delicious!" Annika exclaimed.

Maria dished up the cake and handed each of them a plate. She then stood back a little to watch as they began tasting the delectable chocolate dessert.

Anna Marie took her first bite and rolled her eyes toward James. "This is your mother's chocolate buttermilk recipe."

"Yes." He nodded towards Maria. "I told her this was my favorite dessert, so I got the recipe from my mother, and on special occasions, Maria makes it for me."

"Thank you, Maria, for making this cake. It was also a favorite of mine, and I haven't had it since high school. It's just as I remember. You did a great job!" Anna Marie smiled.

"Wow, I get to try my grandmother's chocolate cake recipe." Annika had been watching her mother and now took a bite with all eyes on her. "I love it! I want the recipe."

James beamed. "I can get that for you. It's a bit different than Mexican chocolate cakes, but you have perfected making it. Thank you, Maria."

Anna Marie could tell how proud Maria was to be able to make this special dinner for them in James' home. The way she acted around him, made it apparent she felt at ease with him. It was obvious she tried her best to take care of him and his home. And now his long-lost love and child would be under her care and protection also.

After lunch, Anna Marie and Annika got up to leave and go back to The Royal Islander.

"I'll have my driver take you back. We can wait out front for him to bring the car around." He motioned toward the massive wooden door, and they followed.

Once outside, everyone was quiet. Probably not knowing what to say next.

"I talked to Michael and Samuel, and they'd like to have a sort of farewell dinner at The Royal Sands Hacienda Sisal restaurant tonight. They have an authentic Mexican dance show after dinner."

"That sounds fun," Annika replied.

"My suggestion is that we all go, including Yvonne, Thomas and Callie." James waited for their answer.

"Mom?" Annika questioned.

"Sounds like a good way to spend our last night." Anna Marie nodded at James.

"Great! I'll make reservations for the group. We should arrive at six since the show starts at eight. Sound, okay?" James smiled at the two women.

"Perfect!" Annika replied.

The black Suburban pulled up, and the driver opened the door for them.

Annika wrapped her arms around James and gave him a huge hug, which was reciprocated by him.

Anna Marie watched as his eyes teared up slightly. She realized he was fighting to control his emotions. He would love his daughter unconditionally.

Annika backed away and got into the car.

James glanced at Anna Marie, and their eyes locked.

She walked towards him, intending to shake his hand and thank him, but found herself wrapped in his arms.

"There's never been anyone else." He whispered in her ear. "I never stopped loving you." James lightly kissed her cheek before releasing her.

A little dazed, she stepped into the Suburban.

CHAPTER 23

ANNA MARIE AND ANNIKA WALKED INTO THEIR ROOM TO FIND A note from Yvonne and Callie on the table.

Meet us at the pool when you get back!

Quickly, they each changed into a swimsuit and headed to the pool. They found Callie in the pool and Yvonne in her pool lounger chair.

"Hey, you guys made it back in one piece!" Yvonne joked.

Annika shed her beach cover-up immediately. "Yup!" she yelled as she jumped in the pool.

Anna Marie set her bag down on an empty chair and spread out her towel on the lounge chair next to Yvonne. Once she was comfortably seated in her chair, she answered Yvonne's question. "I think so."

"Don't know what that means? Was it good or bad?" Yvonne asked.

"I think it went better than anticipated." Anna Marie rolled her eyes.

"Okay, that's good. So, tell me what happened!" Yvonne's face lit up with anticipation.

Anna Marie removed her sunglasses. "At first, I didn't think I was going to make it through the conversation."

"Why?" A look of concern crossed Yvonne's face.

"I had a panic attack. They're scary enough without feeling embarrassed about it," Anna Marie admitted.

"I'm sorry. How did he react?" Yvonne asked.

"He was incredibly caring. He massaged my shoulders till I calmed down, but then I started crying. To my surprise, he wrapped his arms around me and held me for a little while." A slight smile crossed Anna Marie's face.

"Oh. That was good? Right?" Yvonne sat up in her chair.

"Well, it helped, and I eventually calmed down enough that we could have a conversation about the past." Anna Marie gazed toward the pool, where Annika and Callie were also engaged in conversation.

"Great! Did you get to find out his side of the story?" Yvonne couldn't contain her excitement as she swiveled on her chair to face Anna Marie.

"Annika wanted us each to tell our side of the story..." Anna Marie paused for a moment. "She wanted him to go first."

"Did you learn anything that you didn't already know?" Yvonne questioned.

"It seems that we were all simply victims of various unusual circumstances." She hesitated for a moment before continuing, "He didn't get the letter until much later and assumed I'd moved on. And of course, he didn't know about Annika till the other day."

"Was he mad at you?" Deep concern crossed Yvonne's face.

Anna Marie shook her head. "No, he took full responsibility for not coming back or looking for me later."

"Are you still mad at him?" Yvonne asked.

"After listening to his side of the story, it's hard to be mad. He's lost out on a lot, too. So many years lost with Annika. He wants to have a relationship with her." Anna Marie paused slightly. "And me."

"What do you want?" Yvonne asked.

Anna Marie closed her eyes momentarily. "I'm not sure yet. He said he never stopped loving me. But we're older now, we've both built lives without the other. We can't just pick up where we left off."

"No, but you can start over." A smile crossed Yvonne's face. "Spend time together. See if you still like each other and have common interests."

"He has a house in the Denver area and invited us to come out skiing this winter," Anna Marie stated.

"Well, there you go. You both still like skiing. You both obviously like Cancun. You both love flying and work in the industry. And you have a daughter together. Seems like a few important common interests, right there," Yvonne proudly offered.

"It does look that way." Anna Marie knew Yvonne was right.

"And you do find him attractive, right?" Yvonne asked.

"Of course! Who wouldn't? He's definitely a nice-looking man." Anna Marie couldn't help laughing.

"You can say it! He's hot!" Yvonne teased.

Anna Marie couldn't help pretending that wasn't true. "Yvonne!"

"Well, he is, and you know it." Yvonne broke out laughing.

"I haven't dated anyone for such a long time. I don't think I remember what it's like to be with a man, much less have sex with him." Anna Marie's mind reeled with visions of them in each other's arms, kissing and doing many other things in the throes of passion.

"It's a good thing that you've at least thought about having sex with him. I was getting worried about you." Yvonne winked. "But what you want to think about is having him make love to you."

"That means I need to fall back in love with him." The thought of this had her stomach in knots. Was it even possible?

"I don't see that as a problem." Yvonne smiled.

"Oh, I almost forgot we're all having dinner at The Royal Sands' Hacienda Sisal restaurant tonight, and there is an Authentic Mexican Dance show after dinner. James made reservations."

"Sounds fun. So, Thomas will be there?" Yvonne asked.

"It sounded like all eight of us," Anna Marie stated.

"What time?" Yvonne couldn't contain her excitement.

"Six. Annika almost assuredly has already informed Callie," Anna Marie said.

Yvonne glanced over to the girls in the pool. "I'm assuming he'll be sending a car to pick us up?"

"Not sure if he's sending a car or driving his Suburban." Anna Marie could only assume. "We need to be out front at 5:45."

"It's almost 4," Yvonne stated.

"I need to relax a little before we head back up to the room to get ready. It's been a long day already, and it's not nearly done yet." With that, Anna Marie closed her eyes and drifted off.

A half hour later, the four ladies headed up to their room to shower and change into sexy little black dresses and heels for dinner.

Anna Marie only brought a couple of dresses along, thinking she wouldn't even probably wear any of them. Her preference had always been for the black ones, as they tended to accentuate her long blonde hair, so all three were black. She hadn't worn her favorite one yet, so she pulled it out of the closet. This one was more of a sundress style with spaghetti straps and a low neckline. Although it had a snug fit, clinging to every curve of her body. Makeup was applied, and the curling iron had produced loose curls that hung gently down her back. She added a gold necklace, earrings and a bracelet, along with 3-inch heeled sandals.

About five-thirty, Yvonne asked, "Everyone ready?"

All four sun-kissed princesses lined up by the door, nodded, then off they went to their waiting chariot. Suburbans could be considered chariots for the ladies of today. Right?

They arrived at the restaurant to find four men patiently waiting as they exited the SUV. Each guy walked up and took their date by the hand and escorted them inside.

"Anna Marie, you look absolutely breathtaking," James said as he held out his hand to her.

"Thank you." She accepted his outstretched hand and followed him inside the restaurant.

The table James reserved was unquestionably the best one in the house, with a perfect view of the large draped stage. The ceiling was painted a dark navy blue and dotted with silver to mimic the evening sky and stars. Bright yellow and red Mexican motif designs adorned the walls. Once Annika and Callie were seated, they immediately began conversing with Michael and Samuel, while the adults took their seats, but were more of a slow go with conversation.

"I think you ladies will enjoy the show after dinner. The dancers are quite good." Thomas smiled at Yvonne.

The waiter brought out the menus, and everyone became engrossed in picking out what they'd like to eat for their final meal in Cancun.

James stood and walked over to the other end of the table where the young people were seated. "This is my treat, so please choose whatever you'd like." He returned to his seat, then said to Anna Marie, Yvonne and Thomas the same thing, "This is my treat, so please choose whatever you'd like."

Anna Marie chose the giant prawns, Yvonne the Mexican Pasta Special, and the men chose Filet Mignon steaks.

James also ordered one of each appetizer for the whole table to sample. Queso Fundidos, a mixture of Mexican cheeses served with blue corn tortilla strips. Beef Chicharron, crispy cubes of fried beef filets, fresh guacamole, radishes and seared chilies. Octopus Tostadas, crispy tortillas with crunchy octopus served with creamy chipotle sauce and cilantro oil.

Two pitchers of the Sisal's house-made Sangria were brought out, and their glasses were filled.

Anna Marie couldn't help noticing James staring at her and smiling. She couldn't resist bestowing him with a heartfelt smile. Their conversation centered around their parents.

"I'd most definitely like my parents to meet Annika," James said.

"She seemed excited at the thought of having two more grandparents to dote on her. It's up to her, though." Anna Marie glanced toward Annika, but she was deep in conversation with Michael and Samuel.

"How's your schedule when you get back?" James asked.

"I have to check in on Wednesday to bid for my June schedule. How about you?" she asked.

"Me too, but I always pick the same flights. I prefer the Asia routes," he stated.

"Doesn't the jet lag bother you?" Anna Marie asked.

"Not too much. Guess I'm lucky with that." James smiled.

Anna Marie grinned. "Extremely lucky."

"I'd like to come to Minnesota and visit you and Annika. I want to get to know you again. And I'd like to build a relationship with my daughter. Would that be okay with you?" James asked.

Anna Marie stared into his eyes before answering, "Yes, I'd like that."

Immediately, he reached over to hold her hand in his on the table, and she saw his eyes water slightly.

Multiple waiters arrived and served the food moments later. The way everyone immediately began devouring their food, you'd think they hadn't eaten for days. The empty appetizer plates were removed from the table after their glasses were refilled with more Sangria.

The young people opted for the fried ice cream, and the adults did too. Hard to pass up such a delicious dessert option, not readily available in the States, even though it was a common Mexican dessert. Fried ice cream consisted of a hard-frozen scoop of ice cream, coated in a batter and deep-fried, creating a warm, crispy shell around the still-cold ice cream.

After the desserts were brought to the table, festive romantic guitar music played over the speakers, and the ornamental red brocade curtains on the stage opened. The lights dimmed as the additional black lights made stars appear on the walls, ceiling and stage. Dancers filled the stage as women entered, wearing colorful skirts in yellow, red and orange, along with black Mexican-style bolero suits and sombrero hats on the men. Music filled the air as dancers moved and twirled in unison across the stage. Heels clicked when they hit the floor while their fingers snapped together in perfect timing.

The entire table kept their eyes glued to the dancers on the stage.

Anna Marie could sense James watching her. Probably to gauge whether she was enjoying the show. She kept the feelings of dread that she might not see James again, at bay. Even though he'd said he wanted to come to Minnesota, she was afraid he wouldn't. She knew those feelings came from a deep-seated fear from her past. Would she ever see him again? Of course, she would. He would be visiting Annika at the very least, so she was counting on seeing him again. In fact, she found herself wanting to see him. To start a new relationship with him. But was it too soon? They'd only found each other again a week ago. Many people believed that Love at First Sight was a real thing. Maybe their situation was similar. She refocused on the stage when she heard everyone around her clapping.

Way too soon, the show was over, and they were on their way outside to wait for their rides to pull up. She wasn't sure if this would be their goodbye or if James would choose to accompany them back to The Royal Islander. Or simply stop by in the morning to see them off to the airport.

CHAPTER 24

James walked over to stand beside Anna Marie. "I thought maybe we could join you at The Royal Islander for a drink. If that's okay with you?"

"Of course. I'd like that." Anna Marie looked up at him, and a smile spread across her face. He leaned toward her, and she actually thought he intended to kiss her. Then the Suburban pulled up, so he took her hand instead to guide her over toward the group. The door opened and she stepped inside.

This time, James took the seat next to her and closed the door.

"Isn't anyone else riding with us?" she asked.

"I sent two cars to pick up the group, but Thomas decided to drive his car too. Yvonne is riding with him, and the young people are riding in my other car."

"Oh." That was all she had to say. She was now alone in the car with him.

"Did you like the show?" James asked.

"Yes. I've never seen a Mexican Dance show." She couldn't help smiling. "I thought they did an excellent job."

The Suburban pulled out onto the road, and they were on their way back to The Royal Islander. It was only minutes away from The Royal Sands, so they would soon be there. She turned her head to watch the huge hotels all lit up with lights sail by her window. Seemed they were all flying by just like the week had done.

"Anna Marie, is everything all right?" James' tone was serious.

"I'm not sure. I know we just ran into each other a few days ago, but it seems like so much has happened since then. And now I'm leaving tomorrow. And—." She couldn't bring herself to finish the sentence.

James reached for her hand and enclosed it in his. "You'll miss me?"

"I don't know. I'm so confused. This has all happened so fast." She didn't pull her hand away. "I loved you so much before, but you walked away, leaving me with my heart shattered into a million pieces. The scars are still there."

"We were deeply in love, I can't deny that. I was a foolish teenager back then, and didn't realize what we had was special—a love that would last forever. Instead of holding on, I selfishly went off to chase my dreams alone. As an adult, I look back with deep regret, knowing that I totally blew it." He looked into her eyes. "I know that trust is earned and it will take time, but I'm asking you to give us a chance to build a strong relationship based on the love we shared long ago."

"We need to go slow. I'm going to need some time," Anna Marie stated.

"And you don't know what the future holds?" he asked.

"Something like that." She was sure her uncertainty showed, even though she tried to put on a positive face.

"I'm willing to put in all the time you need for us to get there." James smiled and gently squeezed her hand.

The Suburban pulled up at The Royal Islander, and the driver stepped out to open the door for Anna Marie.

James and Anna Marie exited the car and entered through the automatic glass doors into the lobby.

Minutes later, the rest of the group walked through the doors to join them. Annika, Callie, Michael and Samuel were laughing about something and kept walking. "See you guys at the bar," they yelled as they walked out the glass doors leading to the pool.

"You two coming?" Yvonne asked as she and Thomas also walked through the doors.

Alone again. Anna Marie looked at James. "Should we join them?"

His answer was to take her hand and lead her to the door before it closed.

They quickly pushed two tables together and sat down.

James walked over to the bar to talk to the waiter, who followed him back to the table to take their orders. He took a seat next to Anna Marie and Thomas. Music played in the background, the drinks were brought out, and soon the young people were dancing even though there wasn't an actual dance floor. Everyone was having a great time. A slow song played as James led Anna Marie out to the makeshift dance area, where Yvonne and Thomas joined them.

Anna Marie found herself pressed against James' chest. Heat rushed through her body. His hand rested on her lower back. His lips were so near hers. The spicy fragrance of his after-shave surrounded her. She could think of nothing except what it would feel like to be kissed by him. Again. The chemistry between them was off the charts, just as strong as when they were in their teens. Only back then, they didn't have any idea what chemistry even was.

She'd hardly noticed the song ended when she heard James whispering in her ear, "Let's go for a walk." He took her hand as they quickly walked away from the group and passed by the pool to a secluded area on the patio overlooking the ocean. They stood by the railing watching the waves rolling rhythmically to shore, offset by the moon lighting the dark sky.

"I'm going to miss you." James turned to take her into his arms with his hands resting on her lower back. "Will you miss me?"

Anna Marie looked into his blue eyes and saw her future. He was the love of her life, and she realized there was no way she would walk away without giving it her all. "I hate to admit it, but I think I will."

Apparently, that was all he needed to hear. His lips brushed hers gently at first and then deepened into a demanding, soul-searching kiss.

Wrapping her arms around his neck, she leaned into his warm but muscled chest. A fire began burning inside her as passion rushed through her body. Who could walk away from chemistry like this?

His kiss moved to her ear and then her neck.

"Are you sure you have to leave tomorrow?" he asked in a deep voice.

"Yes," Anna Marie hesitantly whispered.

"Anything I can do to change your mind?" James kissed her again. A mind-blowing kiss.

"Maybe you can come to Minnesota. Sooner rather than later," she offered.

"Done deal. I'm looking forward to it." He pulled her in for another kiss. Then took her hand and they slowly walked back to the bar to meet up with the others.

CHAPTER 25

IT WAS JUST PAST MIDNIGHT WHEN THE BAR CLOSED, AND THE group walked into the lobby. Anna Marie watched as Annika gave Michael a quick kiss, with Callie and Samuel doing the same. The girls walked into the elevator. Annika caught Anna Marie's attention, but she wasn't quite ready to leave James yet, so she motioned for Annika and Callie to go up without them.

Only Thomas and Yvonne were still in the lobby, deep in conversation.

"I'd like to take you to the airport tomorrow. What time is your flight leaving?" James asked.

"Not till five. However, we need to arrive at the airport a couple of hours prior, as it's an international flight. So, we need to leave here around two."

"I'll be here around one-thirty." James wrapped his arms around her and kissed her. "I look forward to seeing you tomorrow." He caught Thomas' attention, then motioned toward the door. He slowly released Anna Marie from their intimate hold and walked out the glass doors, followed by Thomas.

"Ready?" Yvonne questioned as she pressed the elevator button.

"Yes." The elevator door opened, and they stepped in.

They walked into their villa to find it in major disarray, with clothes and shoes strewn everywhere.

"Packing, I assume?" Yvonne asked the girls, laughing.

"Of course! What else would we be doing?" Callie answered.

Anna Marie and Yvonne headed to their room to change into pajamas, and soon their bedroom became a chaotic mess as packing began. Everyone laid out what they were going to wear on the plane, along with a swimsuit and cover-up for the morning. It was almost two when they all collapsed on their beds and fell asleep.

James and Thomas each had their drivers take them home. He never drove after having even a couple of drinks. James had a lot on his mind. Mainly Anna Marie. She was such a strong, independent woman. And so beautiful. Made a great life for herself and Annika. Any man would be lucky to have her by his side. He wanted to be that man. He'd spent his whole adult life alone while looking for that special woman who could complete his life. Someone he could share everything with.

Having children was something he hadn't spent much time thinking about. Flying had been his whole life, along with making sure his businesses ran smoothly. Not having time for a family may have been an excuse for becoming a workaholic. What else did he have to spend his time on besides flying and managing the resorts? Nothing. Not a damn thing.

Oh, he'd had a few girlfriends in the past, but nothing that lasted long. Usually, they moved on, claiming that he was married to his jobs, which were more important to him than they were. Unfortunately, they were right. Sadly, none of them had filled the huge hole in his heart left by the loss of Anna Marie. It just hadn't felt the same with them as it had with her. Now was his second chance, and he wasn't about to do anything to screw it up with Anna Marie or Annika.

James hadn't thought he'd ever have any children of his own. He now had Annika, and he intended to build a strong father-daughter relationship with her. Perhaps in the future, there would be grand-children to spoil. His hard work all these years had certainly paid off monetarily, and he had the means to make both Anna Marie's and Annika's lives easier. He could make sure they had all their wants and needs satisfied. They hadn't had much in the past, according to a comment Anna Marie had made about making ends meet. That was about to change because he wanted to make it up to them for not being there for all those years and supporting them. Like a father and husband would've done.

Anna Marie's 40th birthday was coming up in July, which would be the perfect time for a trip to Minnesota. He intended to make sure it was the best birthday she'd ever had. He was going to miss her until then, but there was always the phone, and he would be talking to her. At the very least, once every day until they could be together again.

CHAPTER 26

Anna Marie woke up late, around nine, since they'd all gone to sleep so late. The girls were still sleeping, but Yvonne was already out on the patio having a cup of coffee. She made her way to the shower, the only proper way to wake up in the morning. Yvonne showered next. Eventually, they heard the girls' shower running. They dressed in their swimsuits and threw on their cover-ups.

After the girls were ready, they headed to the pool area to save chairs, then made their way over to the restaurant for the breakfast buffet. So much delicious food. Fresh-cut watermelon, pineapple, and strawberries. Made-to-order coconut and pecan waffles with coconut and caramel syrup, French toast and pancakes. Breakfast sausage and bacon. Fresh-squeezed orange juice and coffee.

They'd opted for a table outside to enjoy the beautiful, warm weather with clear skies. Once back at the table with their filled plates, they began indulging in the scrumptious food.

"How was your vacation?" Anna Marie asked Annika.

"It was great, Mom! Thanks so much. I love this resort. The white sand beaches are so picturesque. Xel-Ha was truly an experience in itself. A few unexpected things happened. One not so good but the other...makes me so happy!" Annika was beaming with happiness.

Anna Marie had tossed out a generic question, not expecting an in-depth answer. But she appreciated it, just the same. Obviously, from Annika's statement, she was thrilled to have had the opportunity to meet James. "I'm glad. Not about the bad part but the rest."

"How about you, Callie?" Yvonne asked.

"I had the time of my life! Except for the one part of course, which was super scary," Callie replied.

"How about you, Mom?" Annika asked.

"It was a great vacation as far as vacations go. Except the scary part." Anna Marie chose not to go into detail about what part she thought qualified as great.

Annika gave her the look. "And what about James?"

"Totally unexpected." She hesitated as they all watched her. "I think I may be open to seeing what happens next."

"Wah Hoo!!!" Annika yelled, and the others clapped their approval.

"And you, Mom?" Callie asked.

"Couldn't have asked for a better vacation than this one with all of you! With the one exception, of course!" Yvonne agreed.

They all laughed and continued eating. When they couldn't eat another bite, they headed to their waiting pool chairs. It was eleven thirty, so they didn't have a lot of time, but they intended to enjoy every last minute they had left.

At about one, they headed back up to the villa for quick showers. Everyone finished packing, put on their makeup and dressed for the trip home. They arrived promptly at one-thirty in the lobby to check out of their villa. Thankfully, they'd been given a late checkout time.

"Here is your receipt, Ma'am," the desk clerk said.

Anna Marie looked it over and realized they hadn't been charged for anything extra that they'd bought. "Are you sure this is correct?"

"Yes, Ma'am. James Olson took care of the extra charges, so everything has been taken care of. You don't owe anything."

"Okay...thanks." Anna Marie continued staring at the receipt.

"I positively like that man," Yvonne said.

"Of course you do." Anna Marie walked over to where the girls were standing with the boys.

"I didn't know Michael and Samuel would be here. Did you?" Yvonne asked.

"No." She observed James and Thomas walk in. "But I knew James was coming." He walked right over to her, gave her a hug, and a quick little kiss. She could see Annika watching out of the corner of her eye. Also in her line of vision was Thomas kissing Yvonne on the cheek.

"I've missed you already," James said.

"It hasn't even been twenty-four hours yet," Anna Marie responded with a coy, flirty smile.

"Here, I want you to take this. It has all my information on it in case you need to get a hold of me," he handed her a business card. "Can I get your phone number? I'd like to be able to call you once you get home."

Anna Marie reached into her purse and pulled out a card with her info on it. Flight attendants don't get business cards, so she'd had some printed on her own. You just never knew when you might need one. Obviously, that hunch had paid off. She handed it to him. "I have this just for you."

James looked it over, seeming to be satisfied that all the info he wanted was on it. "Thanks."

She knew he could get all the info from the resort if he wanted to, but she wanted to give it to him freely.

"Best get going to the airport in case there is traffic." James took Anna Marie's suitcase for her, and they all walked out to the waiting Suburbans.

Yvonne and Thomas rode with Anna Marie and James while the girls were in the other Suburban with Michael and Samuel. It was only a twenty-minute ride to the airport. Once they arrived, the guys helped them get their luggage to the airline check-in counter. After the luggage was checked, it was time to make their way to the gate and say their final good-byes.

"Well, I guess this is it." James kissed her.

It felt like a kiss meant to make sure she wouldn't forget him. Heat rose throughout her body, causing a red flush to encompass her chest and cheeks. Basically, leaving her in a feverish daze.

"I'll be calling tonight to make sure you get home safe." He added another kiss to seal the deal.

Again, her head spun as she trembled a bit. "Okay. Sounds like a plan." Anna Marie kissed his cheek.

"I'm making plans to come to Minnesota. We'll talk about the dates."

Anna Marie looked into those blue eyes that she'd sorely missed all these years. She leaned into him and whispered in his ear, "Don't let me down this time."

"Not a chance. I've learned from my mistakes. Won't happen again." James gave Anna Marie one last soul-searching kiss, then let her go.

She turned and strolled away from him, a little lightheaded and with a soft sigh.

Suddenly, Annika came running back to James as the others kept walking.

Only Anna Marie turned to watch.

Annika hugged James tightly. "I'm so glad I got to meet you. Hope you come to Minnesota!" With that, she ran back to Anna Marie, and they turned away to continue up the escalator to the departure gates.

CHAPTER 27

BY THE TIME ANNA MARIE AND ANNIKA ARRIVED HOME IN Minnesota, it was already ten o'clock that evening. They'd just dragged the suitcases up the steps to their bedroom when the phone rang in the kitchen.

Annika was the closest, so she grabbed it. "Hello."

"You made it home safe, I'm assuming," James said.

"James?" Annika asked.

"Yes, I'm sorry. I should've said that."

Anna Marie came down the stairs and glanced at Annika holding the phone.

"Mom, it's James." She handed the phone to her.

"Hello. I hope I'm not interrupting anything. Just wanted to make sure your flight was good and you made it home safely," James said.

"Yes, it was uneventful. We just got home a little bit ago and now have the task of unpacking." Anna Marie sat down on the couch.

"I can let you go. I can tell you're busy right now," James offered.

"Tomorrow is Sunday, so I don't have to get up early. Can you call back in an hour? It's kinda hectic here right now." Anna Marie held her breath for a moment until he replied.

"Not a problem. If tomorrow would be better, I can do that, too," he offered.

"Later tonight would be good," she said.

"Okay, I'll call you back around eleven. Bye." James ended the call.

Anna Marie placed the phone in the receiver, and her face lit up. *He'd called already!* They were off to a good start.

After unpacking and making sure everything was in order in her house, she locked the doors, turned off the lights and headed up to her bedroom with a glass of wine. Once on the second floor, she peeked into Annika's room, where she was already on the phone, probably with Callie. "Good night," she said softly and closed the door. Makeup off, she slipped into her pajamas and slid into bed, propping up the pillows so she could watch TV until James called back.

Promptly at eleven, the phone rang.

"Hello." She relaxed into the propped-up pillows.

"Anna Marie, hope this is better timing?"

"Definitely. Things are much calmer now that we've unpacked and I'm comfortably lying in bed." She couldn't help giggling like a teenager.

"I think you're teasing me," James joked.

Anna Marie responded, "Maybe. Especially since you are far away."

"Maybe right now, but that can be easily rectified," James laughed.

"Now are you teasing me?" she asked.

"No, I'm dead serious. I could be there tomorrow if that's what you wanted," James offered.

"I have a flight to Seattle on Monday morning. Sorry. How about you? When is your next flight?" she asked.

"I have to be in Denver for a flight on Friday to Japan," James answered.

"This could be tricky. We're going to have to compare schedules to see when we have available free time," she offered.

"I'll email you my schedule tomorrow, then you can send me yours after you find out what flights you'll have after you get your schedule bids back." James summarized, "For the time being, we'll have to settle for talking on the phone."

"Well, that will give us time to get to know each other again so we can see if we have interests in common." She pulled a blanket up to cover her and snuggled under it.

"I think we already know some of them," James stated with confidence.

"We do?" she teased.

"We both love flying and traveling, right?" he asked.

"Yes." Anna Marie smiled, knowing he was right.

"We both like skiing, right?" he asked.

"Yes." Wow, he was going to show her how compatible they would be together.

"I think it's also fair to assume we both like Cancun?" he questioned. "You do, right?"

"Yes, I fell in love with the turquoise water and white sandy beaches the minute I laid eyes on them." Anna Marie envisioned the beach she'd just left.

"Exactly the reason I live here part of the time." A boastful assurance rippled in his voice.

"How much time do you have to spend running the resorts?" she asked.

"We have a highly reliable management team that takes care of the resorts for us." James assured her, "At this point in our lives, the owners aren't usually there for the day-to-day operations."

It was after midnight when James reluctantly said good night to Anna Marie.

The next day, James sent an email to Santos requesting a lunch meeting on Monday. There were some things he needed to know about the incident on the beach. It had all happened so quickly. He wanted to know precisely how his daughter ended up with some low-life street gang member's hands on her, threatening atrocities.

The computer in his office dinged, signaling he had a message. Santos had accepted. They would meet for lunch at the JW Marriott. It was best not to have the conversation at either of their properties.

On Sunday evening, James called Anna Marie at 9, as she'd requested.

"How was your day?" he asked.

"Oh, just an ordinary day in the life of a single parent. Buying groceries, doing laundry, cleaning the house and making dinner."

"Maybe I can help," he offered.

"Do you cook?" she asked.

James couldn't help bragging. "Actually, I'm not a bad cook. I learned a lot from Maria."

Anna Marie chuckled. "She literally took the time to teach you?"

"Clearly, she's an incredibly patient person to have put up with me all these years," he replied.

"When you come to visit, we can try out your cooking skills. Are you any good at grilling?" she asked.

He laughed. "That, I'm very good at!"

The conversation lasted for more than two hours as they talked about everything from the weather to the latest movies they'd seen. Lastly, they set a time to talk every night at nine unless they were flying.

She was slowly getting over her trust issues with each phone call. He was making a strong commitment to build a new, stronger relationship, slowly chipping away at the walls she'd built around her heart to prevent it from being broken again.

Monday, James walked into the JW Marriott to have lunch with Santos. He was shown to a table by the window with a view of the ocean. No one was seated at the tables surrounding them.

"James, good to see you." Santos stood to shake his hand.

"Santos." James took a seat and stared out the window, wondering where he should start this conversation with his old friend.

"It's okay, James, I'd want to talk about the situation if I were you," Santos said.

"I don't even know where to start," James stated.

"We've known each other for a long time. Tell me what you want to know." Santos sat back in his chair and waited patiently.

James wasn't sure where to start. All he could think about was that some lowlife had dared to accost his daughter. "How did Annika end up at your house?"

"Paulo and Diego had their eyes on her and her friend ever since they saw them walking on the beach. You know how it is to be young and foolish. Right? We were that young once, too."

"Yes, but—" James began, but was interrupted.

"Let me finish telling the story," Santos said.

James sat back in his chair to listen and took a sip of his drink.

"The girls and their moms came to the club one night, where the boys saw them." Santos grinned, "Then I assume you sent Michael and Samuel over to keep an eye on them, causing it to become a rivalry between the boys to see who gets the girls."

"My orders were for them to keep an eye on them so they didn't get in any trouble. And these girls were hands off," James stated in a low voice.

"Because Annika was your daughter?" Santos asked.

He felt uncomfortable admitting this to anyone, much less Santos. "Well, yes, except I didn't know it at the time."

"I never knew you had a daughter, James." Santos curiously leaned forward, waiting for an answer.

"Well, that's where the problem lies. I didn't know either. At least not then, anyway." He couldn't hide the pain caused by admitting this.

"How did you not know?" Santos asked.

"It's a long story. Remember my high school girlfriend I talked about when we first met?" he asked.

"Yes. The one who never wanted to see you again. I remember you were quite drunk when you told me that story." Santos smiled.

"Her name was or is Anna Marie. The night before I left, we had sex. Apparently, she got pregnant. Who gets pregnant from having sex once? She had the baby—Annika. She didn't know if I died in Vietnam or what happened to me since I never went back to Minnesota, so she assumed I was dead."

"Wow! That's quite the story. How did they end up at your resort?" Santos asked.

"That is a sheer coincidence and totally by accident." He was beginning to feel at ease with his old friend again.

"Did you know it was her when you saw her?" Santos asked.

"I'd recognize her anywhere." James paused, then continued, "She pretty much hated me for not going back home. She sent me a letter a month after I'd left, saying she never wanted to see me again. She didn't find out she was pregnant until after that. Due to some strange circumstances, I didn't get the letter until four years later, after I got out of the military and was in Colorado." He hadn't told anyone about this, but it felt good to talk with an old friend about his past.

"I'm starting to feel sorry for you, man." Santos took a drink of his whisky.

"Anyway, I didn't find out about Annika until she'd gone missing. Anna Marie didn't know what to do, so she contacted me and finally told me she was my daughter. She was scared and crying. I knew Diego and Paulo were interested in the girls, so I called you." James nodded to Santos, indicating he was now ready to hear what Santos knew about the situation.

"Diego said they ran into the girls on the beach and invited them to the house for some drinks. They were enjoying the sunset and decided to make some dinner. When you called, I was almost home and pulled into the driveway minutes later. So yes, they were eating when I walked in. So, I summoned Diego and Paulo into my office to talk to them. When we came back to the kitchen, the girls were gone. Probably got scared and left to go back to the resort."

"Where did the other guys come into this story?" James asked.

"I could see the panic in Diego's eyes when he saw they were gone." Santos' face grew concerned. "I told him if there was anything else I needed to know, he'd better tell me now. Apparently, a couple of the street gang members had stopped by to threaten Diego and Paulo and ended up making threats against the girls. That's when they took off running after the girls down the beach. I figured I'd better go after them, too, so I followed them."

"What is the status with the street gang members?" James asked.

"They won't bother anyone again." Santos calmly sat back in his chair.

James knew by the look on his friend's face exactly what that meant. They moved in different circles these days, but Santos was still his friend. He wouldn't question that answer. "I owe you, my friend." He nodded to Santos.

"Not for this one. Family is family. Your daughter is family. We take care of our own."

"Thank you, Santos. We will always be friends."

"We will always be family. Let's eat," Santos said, with a wide smile.

They talked about things happening in Cancun while they ate lunch. A couple of hours passed before they each went their separate ways.

CHAPTER 28

James called Anna Marie every night. Their conversations were like reading a book out loud, with each chapter revealing a new page of their lives and connecting them in unexpected ways. Their voices were like a soothing melody, carrying them through the past years of their lives and gently bridging the distance between them. With each word and memory, their bond grew stronger. Finding passions and interests they had in common.

She told him about Annika as a young child, the struggles of raising a teenager, and how proud she was of the young woman Annika had become.

James told her how good it felt to have built, together with his Army buddies, a timeshare dream in paradise, a place where families could escape each year and make lasting memories surrounded by the shimmering, turquoise waters of Cancun. They'd given so many people the chance to experience the paradise they lived in every day.

A couple of weeks later, Anna Marie was in the kitchen when the phone rang. She wondered who was calling since it was too early for James' call. "Hello."

"Hope this isn't a bad time to call," James said.

"Nope. Was just going to sit down and watch some television."

"Great! I wanted to talk to you about coming to Minnesota around the 4th of July for a little over a week. I'll fly in on June 30 and leave on July 10. If that's okay with you?" he asked.

"Let me look at my schedule." Anna Marie set the phone down to get her planner. "Yes, that works. I took that week off since it's the 4th of July holiday. Annika just accepted a job in Marketing with Wells Fargo Bank located at the headquarters in Bloomington. She starts on Monday, July 10, so that will work out perfectly. I think they didn't want to hire someone and then have to pay them for a holiday on the second day."

"Only a few weeks to go, then we'll be together. It's been a while," he stated.

"I'm putting it on my calendar," she said.

"I still have a few loose ends to take care of. I'll call you back later." James hung up the phone.

James had already put his plans in motion for a surprise 40th birthday party for Anna Marie on July 2nd. He'd started planning it with Yvonne a few weeks ago. They'd only needed to confirm his arrival dates. Thomas talked to Yvonne first to see if she'd be willing to help and if it was okay to give James her number. She was ecstatic to have someone help with a birthday party she'd already started planning. They decided to have James invite Anna Marie to dinner, then the rest of the gang—Thomas, Yvonne, Michael, Samuel, Annika, and Callie—would unexpectedly show up. James and Yvonne chose Lord Fletchers on Lake Minnetonka for the location.

James packed for his trip and headed to the Denver airport on the morning of June 30. He was so excited to see her. It had been almost six weeks. Way too long in his book. Through their nightly phone call conversations, he now felt they knew each other remarkably well. Enough to know he wanted to spend the rest of his life with her. The final test would be to see how this week went. He had booked a hotel at the airport for himself, Thomas, Michael and Samuel. Since there was such a large group, he rented a Suburban to drive while in town.

He called Anna Marie when he arrived at the airport.

Anna Marie's phone rang. "Hello."

"Just wanted to hear your voice before I boarded the flight. I can't wait to hold you in my arms again," James confessed. "And kiss you."

"Me, too," she said. "When are the others flying in?"

"They're all flying out of different cities, so I'm not sure. They'll all go straight to the hotel after they arrive," he said.

"Is that what you're doing?" she asked.

"I'm driving straight to your house. After I pick up the rental Suburban, that is. Then I'm taking you out to dinner." He couldn't believe how nervous and excited he felt. He had fallen hard for her. Again. He was in love. Finally, they were going to be together.

"I'll be ready and waiting," she answered.

"The plane is boarding, so gotta go," James said. "See you in a few hours."

"Bye." Seconds later, the phone clicked, indicating the call had ended.

James took his first-class seat. It was great to have such high seniority! He reached into his jacket pocket, pulled out the ring box and opened it. The one-carat diamond solitaire sparkled in the sunlight shining through the window. He couldn't wait to ask her to spend the rest of her life with him. And slide the ring on her finger! He just had to wait for the right moment to propose.

The three-hour flight flew by quickly. Before he knew it, the landing gear was being lowered and the tires hit the runway. He picked up his luggage and waited in line to get his car at the Hertz counter.

"Anna Marie, I'm on my way," James said into the phone after she picked up.

"Okay, you're about fifteen minutes away. See you soon." She ended the call.

James pulled up to a popular back-to-front, split-style house with cedar siding. It was a medium-sized, well-kept home. It was apparent she took good care of it. He parked in the driveway and walked up to the front door. It was a beautiful summer day in Minnesota—a mere 72 degrees. She had the door open so the screen door could let a breeze blow through to the inside of the house. He rang the doorbell just as she walked up to the door and opened it.

"Come in. I need to grab a jacket in case it gets cold later." She left him standing in the front hallway.

James took in all of his surroundings. This was where his daughter had grown up. Nicely decorated with a warm, homey feeling to it. Anna Marie had provided nicely for herself and Annika. An overwhelming sense of sadness washed over him. He'd missed so much. On the hallway table, he spotted a picture of Annika. It looked like her high school graduation picture, which assuredly would be replaced soon with the college graduation picture. His eyes teared up a little. He should've been here. Helping.

Anna Marie stood at the top of the stairs in a teal flirty sundress and heeled sandals. She had a purse and a light sweater in her hands. Truly a vision. She walked down, smiling at him and stopped in front of him.

"You are a splendid sight to behold." He slipped his arm around her and leaned in for a kiss. She melted in his arms as they kissed like two love-starved teenagers. He broke the breathless kiss to say, "I've missed doing this."

"Me, too." She presented him with a smile that lit up her face.

He kissed her again, only a much shorter kiss. "We'd better go for dinner before we end up in your bedroom." She smiled and took his hand after she locked the door they'd just exited.

"I take it you like Suburbans?" she asked as he helped her up into the passenger seat.

After he got in, he replied, "I like them because they hold a lot of people. Which we will need. But otherwise, I much prefer my Corvette."

"Okay, now it all makes sense." She laughed.

"Steak and Ale restaurant, okay?" he asked.

"Great choice." She flashed him a coy smile.

After dinner, James dropped Anna Marie off at her house and walked her to the door.

"Would you like to come in for a little bit?" she asked after unlocking the door.

"I'd love to, but if I did, I don't think I'd want to leave." It felt like her eyes were piercing right through him. He could see how willing her body would be to make that dream of his come true. But he wanted the ring on her finger before that happened. "The guys are arriving soon, and I want to make sure they get in the rooms okay, since they're all under my name." He took her in his arms, pressing her body just slightly against his and kissed her good night. He turned to walk back to the Suburban.

"How about breakfast tomorrow around nine? I'll make pancakes, eggs and bacon," she offered.

He turned back towards her and replied, "I'll be here."

James got into the Suburban and headed to his hotel, where the guys would be waiting for him in the bar. Damn, but he was a goner! He was so in love with her. If it were even possible, he loved her more now than he did in high school.

Anna Marie walked up the stairs to her bedroom and flopped onto the bed. They'd had a wonderful time together at dinner. She was thrilled to see him in person. To be able to touch and kiss him. It would've been nice if he'd stayed a little longer, but in her heart, she knew it was the right choice for him to leave tonight.

Just then, she heard the front door open. "Mom, you home?"

The next morning, Anna Marie and Annika were busy making breakfast together when they saw the Suburban pull up.

Minutes later, Yvonne and Callie pulled up in their Minivan. It was a good thing James had called to say he was bringing guests, thus prompting them to invite Yvonne and Callie. They'd already set up the table outside on the deck for eight people.

Anna Marie set the last dish on the table and sat down at a table filled with her oldest and newest acquaintances. The sun was out, the sky was blue, and it was going to be one of those A+ days weather-wise, with the temperature reaching 80. Everyone was smiling and happy while catching up on what they'd been doing the past weeks since Cancun.

James smiled her way. She couldn't be happier!

That afternoon, they were all going golfing at The Wilds Golf Course in Prior Lake, courtesy of James. It had been a long time since she'd golfed, and Annika had only golfed once but was eager to give it a shot. From what she'd heard, James and Thomas were avid golfers. The boys were also pretty good, but were willing to help teach the ladies.

Her 40th birthday was the next day, Sunday, and no one had said a word about it. She felt confident that Annika knew the date along with Yvonne and Callie, so she figured that maybe they'd planned something as a surprise. She couldn't lie though, she would indeed be disappointed if everyone had forgotten.

Before she knew it, the day was almost over. They'd enjoyed burgers at a little local place, Lions Tap, for dinner. Her heart went out to Annika, who had thoroughly enjoyed having James help her with her golf swing. There was so much pride in her face that she finally had a dad, and it appeared he wanted to be there for her.

James brought everyone back to her house. He walked into the house with Anna Marie. Yvonne and Callie left for home while Annika and the guys waited outside for him, since he was the driver.

Once inside, he took her hand in his. "Anna Marie, if I'm remembering correctly, I know it's been a long time, but tomorrow is your birthday, right?"

"Yes. It's a big one. I'm going to be officially old." She smiled as she admitted it.

"Never as old as me." He laughed.

"Right. Your birthday is in January."

"Yes. I'd like to take you to dinner tomorrow night at Lord Fletchers on Lake Minnetonka, if that's okay with you? Just the two of us." He waited for her reply,

"It's perfect. Thank you." She smiled.

"I have some business to attend to tomorrow, so can I pick you up at five?" he asked.

"I'll be ready," she said.

Once again, he kissed her briefly at the front door and left. She completely understood, as Annika was just on the other side of the door. They desperately needed to find some place where they could be alone.

It was so hard to walk away from her. James had wanted nothing more than to stay.

In the morning, he was meeting Annika to pick up the cake. He'd already purchased his gift for her. Annika was in charge of putting together a picture board of Anna Marie's life, which he'd offered to help with. She had all the pictures and the board, so all he had to do was help her attach them with double-stick tape. So, Anna Marie wouldn't know about it, they were putting the project together at Yvonne's house.

A project with his daughter. He couldn't wait.

CHAPTER 29

Annika disappeared the next morning. "I've got some errands to run. Catch you later, Mom." She ran out the door, not giving Anna Marie a chance to say anything.

She tried calling Yvonne but got no answer. Since it seemed like everyone had ditched her, she decided to go shopping for a new dress to wear for her fancy birthday dinner at Lord Fletchers. It took the whole afternoon to find the perfect one and matching shoes, of course. When she got back home, Annika was still gone. It was so not like her. And so not like Yvonne to not have called her back. She was sure they had something up their sleeves for a surprise tonight.

She spent extra time with her makeup and hair. Slipped on her new black sleeveless dress and black strappy high heels at quarter to five. One last look in the mirror to make sure she was happy with what she saw. Now she only hoped James did, too.

A few minutes before five, the doorbell rang. She opened the door and saw James in a black suit. He was so handsome, maybe even more so than in high school. Absolutely, more distinguished and sophisticated now.

He opened the screen door and stepped inside. "You are stunningly beautiful." He couldn't help himself and leaned in for a quick kiss. "We should go, so we're not late for our reservation."

It was a forty-five-minute drive to Minnetonka in rush hour traffic. When they arrived, he drove up in the valet line and helped her out of the Suburban by taking her hand. Even though it was Sunday, it was already busy, most likely due to the holiday week, with so many people taking the whole week off for the 4th of July.

James stepped up to the hostess stand to check on their reservation, then motioned for her to join them. They followed the hostess through a couple of rooms and up a few stairs to a private room overlooking the lake. It seemed like an overly large room for the two of them as she walked over to look out the window.

"Surprise!" Annika, Yvonne, Callie, Michael, Samuel and Thomas all yelled from behind her as they rushed into the room and began hugging her.

"I bet you thought I forgot." Annika hugged her. "Happy Birthday, Mom!"

Next, Yvonne and Callie were hugging her and said, "Happy Birthday, Anna Marie!"

Then the guys made their way over to wish her a Happy Birthday. The serving staff brought in another table and set it quickly. More servers carried the chairs into the room. An extra table was brought in, and another server carried in a cake, which he placed in the center. A table sitting in the back of the room was brought closer.

Annika proudly placed a project board filled with pictures of Anna Marie through the years.

"Mom, come and look! I made this for you with a little help from James."

She walked over to the table and checked out all the photos. With a sniffle, a tear slipped down her cheek. "I love it! Thank you!" She hugged Annika tightly.

Yvonne placed a couple of photo albums on the table, filled with pictures of all four of them through the years.

Callie set the gift bags on the table.

James stood back, watching intently a few feet away.

She smiled and strolled towards him. "Did you have anything to do with this little surprise party?"

"I've missed so many, I was glad to celebrate this one with you and throw this little party."

"It's wonderful. Thank you." She reached up to give him a quick kiss, but found herself lingering minutes longer than anticipated.

Finally, he broke the kiss. "Ready to eat?"

She nodded. He took her hand as they walked over to the table and sat down, where their friends joined them. The waiter appeared and handed them all menus. After they'd ordered, bottles of wine were brought out—Red, White and Blush. James had ordered appetizer sampler trays for the whole table to try, which arrived after the wine. It was a lively conversation with everyone joining in. The food was served. They all enjoyed the delicious meals of lobster, steak, shrimp, scallops, along with various side dishes of baby red potatoes, mashed potatoes, rice and fresh broccoli.

After dinner, it was time for the cake. It was chocolate with chocolate buttercream frosting, decorated with ruby-red roses, and it looked delicious. The servers brought the cake over to set it in front of Anna Marie. A vase filled with twelve long-stemmed roses had been placed on the table next to the cake. Tactfully, only four candles had been placed on it. The roses were moved over to the center of the table. Once the candles were lit, she made a wish and blew them out. Everyone joined in singing *Happy Birthday*.

The waiters cut the cake and served everyone a slice.

While they enjoyed their dessert, the photo albums made their way around the table. The ladies shared stories about the pictures with the guys. The servers cleared away the dessert plates while Annika and Callie brought the gift bags over and set them in front of Anna Marie.

"I suppose you want me to open these?" She laughed.

"Of course, Mom!" Annika said.

The first gift she opened was a photo album filled with their

Cancun vacation pictures. "Yvonne and Callie, thank you. I will treasure this." She held the book up against her chest to show how much it meant to her.

The next gift was a charm bracelet with a mother-daughter charm from Annika. "I love it! Thank you!" She immediately put it on her wrist and held it up for all to see.

The next gift was from the guys—Thomas, Michael and Samuel. The large bag held a medium-sized black leather Prada purse. The ladies all oohed and aahed over the purse. "Thank you, guys! Never thought I'd own a Prada. I love it!"

James pulled a small wrapped box out of his suit coat pocket and handed it to her. She took the box from him and made eye contact. Her stomach tightened as she was unsure what was in it. *Would he propose to her like this?* She hoped not. That should be done privately. But the question she kept asking herself was, would she accept? Absolutely! She was head over heels in love with him. Possibly, they could have a rare second chance to have a life together.

Carefully, she opened the gift, tearing the paper off, then slowly opened the box. Inside was a striking red ruby pendant set in gold on a gold chain. She held it up for all to see, then turned toward James. "Thank you. I love ruby stones, they're my birthstone." She leaned over and kissed him. "Can you help me put it on?" She handed it to him so he could fasten it around her neck.

The conversation flowed around the table for another hour before they rounded up all the stuff they'd brought and headed to the cars. Anna Marie and James drove back to her house while the rest headed to the hotel to drop off the guys. Annika rode along knowing Yvonne would drop her off at home on the way back.

This time, when they arrived at the house, James went inside with her. As soon as the front door closed, he took her in his arms. "Did you have a good birthday?"

"Best one ever! Thank you for all that you did." His lips were so close to hers without touching. She couldn't stand it anymore and pressed her lips against his.

He responded immediately, deepening the kiss. His hand moved slowly up and down her back, sliding smoothly over the satiny fabric of her dress. He broke the kiss momentarily. "I love you, Anna Marie. I never stopped."

"I love you too." She wrapped her arms around his neck and kissed him again. Their chemistry was undeniable.

"I'd like nothing more than to make love to you right this moment," he told her. "But we have to do this right this time. Plus, our daughter could walk through that door at any moment." He never released her from his arms, but grinned at her. "What is the plan for tomorrow?" He gently brushed a strand of hair from her face.

"Grocery shopping?"

James laughed. "Really?"

"We need food for the barbecue on the 4th, which is Tuesday, don't we?"

"I did promise you I knew how to grill, didn't I?" he asked.

"Yes, you did." She bestowed a huge smile on him.

"Okay, I'm going with you. What time should I be here?" he asked.

"One?" she shrugged.

James kissed her cheek. "What is the plan for after the groceries?"

"Maybe a movie night?" She leaned against him.

"That sounds like fun. Steak dinner?" he kissed her other cheek.

"I can work with that." She brushed her lips against his ever so lightly.

He couldn't resist any longer, so he kissed her one more time before walking to the door. One of those long, sensual kisses. "See you tomorrow."

"Tomorrow." She slowly closed the door.

Five minutes later, Annika walked in.

CHAPTER 30

JAMES AND ANNA MARIE ARRIVED AT THE GROCERY STORE
shortly after one. They picked up steaks, potatoes and salad for
dinner. Then hamburgers, brats, chips, potato salad and watermelon
for the 4th of July.

Anna Marie and Annika had already made the desserts for both
days that morning. Brownies, Magic Bars, and Chocolate Chip
Cookie Pies.

Yvonne, Callie and the guys were coming over at six. From Anna
Marie's extensive DVD library in the family room, he picked out the
new James Bond movie, Golden Eye, just released on DVD, to watch
later. Then he set out the bowls for the must-have movie popcorn.
Everything was ready to start cooking around five, so James and Anna
Marie filled their wine glasses with Chardonnay and sat out on the
deck to relax until their guests arrived.

A few hours later, they were all seated at the patio table, enjoying
their steak dinners and wine.

James stood up to make a toast. "To friends and family. Thanks
for sharing this beautiful day with us." They all joined in the toast.
Soon, the air was filled with laughter and conversations. The sun was

in its final stage, slipping behind the horizon, when the mosquitoes began appearing. They quickly moved inside to the family room.

After everyone was comfy on the couches and chairs with their popcorn and drinks, James popped the DVD in, and the movie started. Anna Marie snuggled into James on the couch for the whole movie.

After the movie credits rolled across the screen, Yvonne and Callie drove the guys back to the hotel before heading home. Annika had already said her goodbyes and carefully navigated the stairs to her bedroom, half asleep. James was the last to leave after showering Anna Marie with kisses on his way to the door. "I'll be seeing you in my dreams tonight." A huge grin crossed his face as he closed the door behind him.

Finally, the 4th of July had arrived, and all her guests would be there any minute. The bean bag game was set up in the backyard, ready to go.

Michael helped Annika set up music speakers outside. The food was already prepped for the grill.

On her way to the kitchen, carrying empty trays inside, Anna Marie paused to look back at the table where everyone was enjoying the food. By the time she came back outside, Michael and Samuel were busy tossing the bean bags and cheering each other on. Soon, the evening was closing in. *Where had the afternoon gone?*

It was time for the evening festivities now. They all piled into the cars with blankets and chairs, then headed to Sandy Point beach on Prior Lake to watch the fireworks. Many people had already arrived, but they managed to find a good spot to set up their chairs. The sky was clear, filled with bright stars, while the temperature was in the low seventies.

Fortunately, the city had sprayed the park for mosquitoes so they wouldn't be eaten alive! Although she'd brought the mosquito spray along, just in case. The chairs were arranged in two rows of four. Anna Marie and Yvonne's chairs were next to each other, as were Annika and Callie's. Of course, the men and boys were all seated next to their ladies. Finally, the sky lit up with sparkling red, gold, green and blue from all the fireworks.

James reached over to hold her hand. "These are beautiful. I remember when we spent the 4th of July together in high school with our friends. This reminds me of that. Do you remember?"

Anna Marie squeezed his hand slightly. "Yes, I remember. Somehow, this time seems different. Better, somehow."

When the fireworks were over, they loaded the chairs back in the Suburban and parted ways for the night. Yvonne and Callie drove the guys back to the hotel, then went home. James, Anna Marie and Annika returned to the house and unloaded the chairs, which they put in the garage.

"James, I totally enjoyed spending the 4th with you and Mom. Thanks for being here." Annika hugged him quickly, then ran downstairs to her room. "Good night," she yelled back at them.

"I should get going back to the hotel. Tomorrow, I'd like to spend time with you, just the two of us. If you're interested." James wrapped his arms around her waist and kissed her. After a long, breathless kiss, he pulled back.

"I'd love to." She replied a bit breathlessly as her lips felt so warm from the kiss. "What time should I be ready?"

"I thought we'd go out to Stillwater for the day. How does noon sound?" he asked.

"Perfect." She gifted him with a beautiful smile that lit up her face.

"Bring a dress along to change into for dinner later." He gave her a somewhat wickedly sexy grin. "We're having dinner at Jax Café in downtown Minneapolis."

"Got it." Anna Marie couldn't help smiling at him. "We went there for the senior prom. I'll be ready."

James gave her another quick kiss and then left.

Anna Marie walked upstairs to her bedroom to get ready for bed, where she could spend the whole night dreaming about him.

Thankfully, she'd picked up two dresses when she'd gone shopping the other day, because she certainly didn't want to wear the same dress as the other night. It could often be challenging to find the perfect dress, so when she'd found two, there was no alternative but to buy both. It just so happened that the other one was a deep ruby red color that would be perfect with her new ruby pendant necklace.

Bright sunlight streamed into her bedroom as she woke up around eight. The house was quiet, so she knew Annika was still asleep. The shower was calling to her.

Twenty minutes later, feeling completely refreshed, she chose a tan pair of shorts and a black tank top. It was going to be a beautiful sunny day in the low eighties. She pulled out a jean jacket, just in case they ended up somewhere where the air conditioning was set to cold.

The red dress and black heels were on the bed. She placed them into a garment bag along with a black shawl and a small black evening bag. In another bag, she put her makeup, a comb, and hairspray. She was now ready to spend the day with James. This day had been a long time coming. A day where they could be alone. To just be themselves and have some plain old fun.

The shower could be heard running, which meant Annika was up. She went down to the kitchen to have a bagel and some orange juice. Sitting at the table reading the local newspaper, she heard Annika running up the stairs.

"Mom?"

"In here," Anna Marie answered.

Annika plopped down in the chair beside her. "What's the plan for today?"

"James is picking me up at noon and we're going to spend the day in Stillwater. Afterwards, we're going to dinner somewhere fancy. So, you're on your own for today."

"That's fine, I was planning on showing Michael around Minneapolis today anyway." She poured a bowl of cereal, topped it with milk, then sat down in the chair on the opposite side of the table. "My mom has a date? Never thought I'd be able to say that!"

"I thought I taught you to *never say never?* Perfect example right there!" They both broke out laughing.

Her garment bag and another large, soft-sided bag with makeup, shoes, and other things she might need sat in the front hallway, waiting.

James arrived promptly at noon.

"Mom, he's here!" Annika had been watching out the window for his Suburban to pull up. She opened the front door seconds after the doorbell rang. "She'll be down in a couple of minutes. Come in."

"Hope it's all right if I steal your mom for the day?" James watched for her response.

"I don't think it's up to me. She makes her own decisions. Always has. And I feel pretty confident she'll be in safe hands with you." Annika smiled at him.

Anna Marie walked down the stairs, carrying her jean jacket and sunglasses. She flashed James a brilliant, beautiful smile. "I think I'm ready." She picked up her purse, James grabbed the bags, and they walked out to the Suburban.

"Have fun!" Annika yelled after them and closed the door.

James and Anna Marie got into the Suburban. Thirty minutes later, they pulled onto Stillwater's Main Street to look for a parking spot. Antique stores, art galleries, boutiques, restaurants and bars lined the street with the St. Croix River just a block away. They stopped in a few stores to browse, then walked down a couple of blocks to the Freight House restaurant, complete with a large outdoor wooden deck area facing the river. Built in 1883, the building was placed on the National Registry of Historic Sites in 1979.

Loaded nachos and raspberry lemonades proved to be the perfect lite lunch. Warm weather and clear skies always seemed to bring out the boaters and jet skiers in large numbers. The river was shared with the larger yachts and even bigger paddleboat ships.

"I realized I'd never been here and wanted to see it for the first time with you." James smiled.

"Thanks. I've only been here a few times. Stillwater's historic side is evident in the buildings from the 1800s and the *somewhat* secret caves used by gangsters during the Prohibition Days to store bootlegger liquor supplies," Anna Marie related from what she'd read about it.

"Caves? That sounds interesting. We might have to check that out another time," James suggested.

"There are a couple of companies offering tours. You have to make reservations, though, so I'm sure they're currently sold out since the crowds are large today." Anna Marie sipped her raspberry lemonade and gazed out toward the shimmering water of the river.

After lunch, a walk along the river seemed fitting, so they strolled all the way down to the marina next to the biker bar, P D Pappy's.

James studied the boats in the marina. "I have to admit, I'd forgotten what a large boating state Minnesota is, but it's surprising to see so many small yachts lined up in the Marina."

"Yes, the smaller yachts are particularly common in Stillwater, Lake Minnetonka and Lake Superior. You've been gone a long time." She gazed out at the yachts lined up in rows in the boat slips.

"I'd really like to spend more time here in Minnesota." He turned to face her.

"I'd like that, too." She moved closer to him.

James kissed her, and she welcomed his kiss by melting in his arms. After the sweet kiss, he reached for her hand while they walked back to the car, holding hands.

Around four, they left Stillwater and headed to his hotel to change clothes.

He parked the Suburban, and they headed up to his room with her bags in tow. The elevator at the Hilton opened on the eighth floor, and they exited. She followed him down the hall to the end, where he opened the door to a suite. Along with a separate bedroom, there was a living room, dining room and kitchen bar area. Two bathrooms, too.

"You can change in the bedroom. I'll grab my suit and change in the other bathroom," he stated with a grin.

Anna Marie stood alone in his massive hotel bedroom, wondering exactly what she'd gotten herself into. Could she get used to his lifestyle? She hoped so, because she was completely head-over-heels in love with him. She loved him in high school, but this felt totally different. If that was even possible. This was adult love. Complete love. Forever love.

She opened her bag, walked into the bathroom to freshen up her makeup, then curled her hair. One last look in the mirror after she slipped on her dress and three-inch heeled sandals. She wanted to impress him, and she hoped he would like what he saw.

When the bedroom door opened, James couldn't believe his eyes. She looked breathtaking in her strapless red satin dress that hugged every inch of her body. Her long, tanned legs were flawlessly displayed under the short dress. Long blonde curls flowed gently down her partially bare back. She was sheer beauty. The thought crossed his mind to propose right here and now, then simply order room service. But she'd waited over twenty years for his proposal, and he wouldn't deny her a proper one.

He closed the gap between them, quickly wrapping her in his arms and kissing her. She kissed him back, and the chemistry ignited a fire that would burn forever between them. When the kiss ended, he took her hand in his and they left the room.

They arrived at Jax Café thirty minutes later, where he valet-parked the Suburban at the door. He'd made a reservation for six-thirty, and they were shown to a private outside patio off to the side of the main one. It was still light out since the summer sunset wouldn't happen until almost nine. The waiter immediately brought out a bottle of White Zinfandel and poured each of them a glass.

"This is so romantic, James. Good choice for dinner." She noticed they didn't have any menus.

"I took the liberty of ordering for us ahead of time. Steak and Lobster. It's their specialty. Hope that's okay with you?" James watched for her response.

"This lady will never pass up lobster!" she answered with a laugh.

Lobster bisque was served first, along with fresh bread. Then dinner was served.

Anna Marie smiled at him. "I've only been here one time. That was a long time ago. With you. I've heard this place is still known for its exceptional food. I have to say the food has been delicious."

"I checked around at the hotel, and Jax still came highly recommended. Glad you like it," he said.

After the meal, two small molten chocolate cakes adorned with fresh raspberries and a dab of fresh whipped cream were served for dessert. The dishes were cleared as soon as they finished indulging in the chocolate decadence.

James now felt nervous as he stood up, taking her hand so she would stand up in front of him. He could see the confusion in her eyes. He just needed to do it. Now! "Anna Marie, I have loved you since we were teenagers. Never stopped loving you, even though we had gone our separate ways. Meeting you again in Cancun was certainly fate putting us back where we belonged. Together. We have missed so much time, but we are still young and have a lot more of life to live. I have totally fallen for you again as the strong, independent woman and mother you've become. I want to spend the rest of my life with you at my side. And also, as a family with Annika." He bent down on one knee in front of her, pulled the ring box out of his pocket and removed the ring. "Anna Marie, will you do me the honor of spending the rest of your life with me and marrying me?"

Her excitement was monumental as a smile spread across her face, and her eyes sparkled in the low lights surrounding them. "Yes. I've waited so long for this moment. Yes!"

He rose, slid the ring on her finger, and wrapped his arms around her waist as their lips met in a passionate kiss. In the background, they heard clapping and cheers from the other people seated on the patio.

Finally, they broke the kiss.

A waiter appeared with two glasses of champagne. They accepted the glasses and sat back down at their table.

Anna Marie couldn't take her eyes off the sparkling new diamond engagement ring on her finger.

After they took a few sips of their champagne, the waiter appeared with the bill, and James handed him a credit card.

Minutes later, they were outside waiting for the valet to bring up the Suburban. James opened the passenger door for her to get in, then he walked to the driver's side and got in.

Shifting the car into drive and exiting onto the street, he asked, "Where to now?"

"What do you mean?" she asked.

"Your house or the hotel?" James prompted.

"I say the hotel," Anna Marie stated boldly.

"Are you sure?"

"Yes." Her answer was definitely emphatic.

James grinned at her.

They discussed dinner, the proposal and her ring on the drive back to the hotel.

"We need to plan a wedding," James said.

"When do you think would be the appropriate time?" she questioned.

"Valentine's Day on the beach in Cancun?" James tossed out there.

"I love it! That's perfect!" Anna Marie beamed with excitement as she stared at the ring.

After parking the Suburban, they walked hand in hand into the hotel lobby to catch the elevator.

Once inside his suite, she dropped her purse on a chair and kissed James like there would be no tomorrow. His arms were around her, pressing her body tightly against his. The fires smoldering inside each of them for way too many years came to life, burning fiercely as the chemistry between them exploded.

She pulled away slightly, then turned to walk into the bedroom. Stopping to glance back at him, she lifted her long hair away from the dress' zipper. He eagerly unzipped it. She slowly turned toward him and allowed the dress to slide down to the floor, then stepped out of the red fabric at her feet. She only wore a strapless bra and skimpy underwear. Oh, and her high-heeled sandals.

Removing his suit jacket, he unbuttoned his shirt as his eyes seemed to burn through her. "This night has been long anticipated."

With a silent nod of her head, Anna Marie could see the passion in his gaze. She could feel the heat from his eyes along her now flushed skin, piercing down to her very soul.

He wrapped her in his arms, and they fell backward onto the bed while entwined in each other's arms. "I've imagined this night in my mind many times over the years. Let's make it a reality. I love you so much, Anna Marie."

"I love you, James." She kissed him and knew this would be a night she would remember forever.

EPILOGUE

Valentine's Day Wedding

Anna Marie and Annika arrived in Cancun on February 12 to take care of a few last-minute preparations before the wedding. James had taken care of the venue, which would be at The Royal Islander on the beach. She was, of course, worried about the weather not cooperating, but there was nothing any of them could do about that except to have a contingency plan ready just in case. That plan meant it would be moved inside if it rained. He'd told her not to worry, he had it all taken care of.

They were all staying at the resort rather than at his house. He'd reserved eight penthouse villas in the same building for the wedding party. She wasn't sure they would need that many, but he wanted to be sure they had plenty of rooms in case they needed them. Not many people would be coming from the States, except for a few of their airline friends who could fly free standby, including their parents.

Sally, who had unintentionally brought Anna Marie and James back together again, would be at the wedding. James, of course, had friends in Cancun who would be coming. As for the problem of others not being able to make the trip, they planned a reception in Minneapolis in June at Lord Fletcher's for their Minneapolis and Denver friends.

Anna Marie stood on the balcony of her villa, gazing out at the turquoise water of the ocean in the Gulf of Mexico. *I'm so lucky to be standing here!* She heard the door open, and she assumed it was James. He walked in and stood beside her at the railing, putting his arm around her.

"Everything alright?" he asked.

"Perfect. Just thinking about how lucky I am to be here. With you!" She turned and kissed him.

After a couple of heat-inducing minutes of the kiss, he let her up for air. Smiling at her, he said, "There are just a few last-minute items we have to take care of. The baker has dropped off a sample cake for you to taste. And the florist sent over a couple of flower photos and a small sample to make sure they create exactly what you are anticipating."

"Okay. Where is the cake?" she asked.

"They will bring it up shortly, along with the photos and samples that were dropped off. Anything else we need to take care of?" he asked.

"Nope. We brought the dresses and accessories with us. You have the photographer lined up, right?" she asked.

"Taken care of. I booked a videographer, too. The Royal Islander DJ will take care of the dancing music, and Jorge Duran will be playing during the wedding." James kissed her cheek.

"Great! And the pastor? Did you find one?" she asked.

"Pastor Johnson is arriving tomorrow," he said.

"My pastor? He's coming to Cancun? How?" She covered his face with kisses.

"I offered to pay his expenses and gave him a complimentary stay at The Royal Islander for a week," James said.

"You mean like when you gave me and Sally those vacation packages?"

James laughed. "Not the same thing. I wanted to have you for my own again. I don't feel that way about the pastor, thank you very much."

Anna Marie was practically jumping for joy as she hugged and kissed him.

"The chef is preparing a seafood feast for the reception and making the ice sculptures himself." He beamed at her.

"Did you come up with something for the bachelor and bachelorette parties?" she asked.

"Yes. The JW Marriott has a VIP club room with a DJ. We could combine them with the rehearsal dinner. If that's okay with you?" he asked.

"I suppose you are friends with the manager there, right? I think that's a great idea!" She showered him with light kisses. "Did I ever tell you that you are everything I've ever wanted in a man?" She wrapped her arms around him and smiled.

"No," he answered. "But my goal is to always be there with you for whatever you need for the rest of our lives." He hugged her tightly and kissed her neck lightly, trailing kisses along the way up to her lips.

The rehearsal went off without a hitch, and the dinner at the JW Marriott was served in a private room on the VIP Club floor. Both sets of Annika's grandparents chose to return to The Royal Islander after dinner, leaving the younger people to have fun dancing the night away at the Club. Anna Marie and James walked them down to the lobby to make sure they safely got into the Suburban with James' driver.

Afterwards, the rehearsal dinner attendees headed into the Club to dance the night away. James held Anna Marie close to him as they slow danced to Prince's *Purple Rain*, a song she'd requested.

She leaned up to whisper in his ear. "Thank you. Everything is perfect."

"I'm glad I succeeded. My goal is to make your dreams come true."

On Valentine's Day, Anna Marie woke up to a bright sunny day. That alone brought a smile to her face. She loved the sun! This was a day she had given up dreaming about years ago. She was getting married today! To a man she'd fallen in love with as a teenager. Fate had dealt them a fatal blow back then that she almost hadn't survived. But ultimately, with the help of her parents and her own determination, she'd made a life for herself and her daughter. They'd missed out on many things, but they had each other and the necessities of life.

Just when she'd thought she'd be alone, after Annika left to start her own life with a new job, fate had intervened again to bring James back into her life. She wasn't sure whether it was just fate or God, but she felt incredibly thankful to have him back in her life and for them to have this second chance at love.

She wouldn't see James until the wedding today. They'd decided to be old-fashioned in that old custom of not seeing the bride till she walked down the aisle. The wedding started at four. Today would be a girl's pamper day. Her mother, James' mother, Annika, Yvonne and Callie were all meeting at the breakfast buffet at ten, before heading to the spa. They'd be enjoying a massage, mani-pedis, then showering before heading up to her room, where six hair stylists would be doing their hair updos. She couldn't stand to go anywhere without a shower first, so it looked like she'd be taking two showers today.

Anna Marie sat in front of the mirror in the bathroom after her second shower, while the stylist did her magic with her long hair, forming ringlets that hung down in the back. Afterwards, she applied her makeup. Next, the jewelry. It wasn't traditional to wear red for a wedding, but she chose to wear the exquisite ruby pendant necklace James had given her for her birthday. He knew she would be wearing it, so this morning, a small gift box had arrived with matching ruby earrings, which she now put on.

Annika walked in wearing her red spaghetti-strapped, sleek satin bridesmaid dress. "Wow, Mom! Those are beautiful!"

"Well, he sure has great taste!" Anna Marie said.

"I'm so happy for you, Mom. I know you've waited a long time to get married." Annika sat down on a chair.

Anna Marie could see Annika's eyes tearing up a little. "Everything okay?"

"It's a happy day for me, too. I will now have a mom and dad." A tear escaped and rolled down her cheek.

"Oh, honey, don't cry. You'll mess up your makeup. It's a happy day for all three of us! Come here." Anna Marie handed her a tissue.

Mother and daughter hugged and laughed.

"Everyone ready in here?" Yvonne walked into the bathroom. "It's time to get this show on the road, as they say! Men are waiting on us!"

Down at the beach, floorboards had been placed over the sugar-fine white sand. Rows of white chairs were lined up in front of a white wooden gazebo with an arch covered in white and red flowers —mainly roses. Separate boards were placed on each side of the arch for the wedding party, along with another walkway path down the center for the bride to walk down. The weather cooperated with clear blue skies and a soon-to-be setting sun.

Finally, the bridesmaids were escorted to the gazebo by the groomsmen.

Anna Marie's dad stood at the end of the path as she walked up to take his arm. Now it was her turn.

"Ready?" her dad asked.

"I've been waiting my whole life for this day. Let's do it!" Anna Marie beamed.

"Me, too." He smiled and held out his arm to her.

She took his arm and they walked up the aisle, now covered in red rose petals.

James eagerly waited for her while grinning from cheek to cheek.

A smile spread across her face. She knew he loved her, and she loved him.

It seemed like a much longer walk than it actually was. At last, she arrived at the gazebo to take James' arm. Now they both walked over to where Pastor Johnson stood waiting.

Soon they were exchanging vows and placing rings on each other's fingers.

"I have and will love you forever," James said.

"I have and will love you forever," Anna Marie said.

"You may now kiss the bride," the pastor announced.

James took Anna Marie into his arms and gave her a swooning kiss, to which the crowd clapped loudly.

They walked back down the aisle together as man and wife. It had only taken them a mere twenty-some years to get there, but they'd eventually made it. Wasn't there a saying that went something like—*better late than never?*

The rest of the night was somewhat of a blur except for a slow dance to *Can't Help Falling in Love* by Elvis Presley. It seemed to be the perfect song for them, and she felt so right being held in his arms.

Hours later, they snuck out and climbed into James' Suburban to spend their wedding night at the JW Marriott's presidential suite. No one knew where they were off to, and that was how they wanted it. Lying in the massive king-size bed, they made love and fell asleep in each other's arms. They slept in until nine and ordered room service for breakfast. Pancakes covered in fresh strawberries, topped with whipped cream, along with bacon and eggs.

James leaned over to lick a bit of cream from her lip. "I love you."

He couldn't resist kissing her thoroughly, so he did. After he pulled back, he grinned at her.

"I can't believe we're actually married and I get to see you every day. I love you so much." She kissed him back.

Just then, the room phone rang. "Who would be calling us right now?" James picked up the phone.

"Hi, are you two awake yet?" Annika asked.

"Yes, we are," he replied. "Wait...how did you know where we were?"

"Can't tell you. I've been sworn to secrecy!" She laughed.

"What can I do for you?" he grinned as he asked.

"You know that flight you guys are booked on to Denver at six?" she asked.

"Yes, what about it?' he questioned.

"We're all crashing your honeymoon. We are on the same flight. Looking forward to skiing with my dad!" Annika stated calmly, then burst out laughing.

"Anna Marie, did you know about this?" he asked.

She shook her head. "Guess it'll be a family and friends' honeymoon."

James laughed. "See you all at the airport, then." He hung up the phone.

"Dang, how I love you!" Anna Marie said, laughing along with him.

"And, I love you," James replied. "But right now, I have you all to myself. So, I'm going to shower you with kisses and anything else your heart desires until we have to leave this room."

"Oh, I finally got what my heart desired, but I sure hope you got a late check out!" Anna Marie fell back on the bed to enjoy the kisses and whatever came next.

Not the end, but the beginning of their love and adventure story for many years to come!

AUTHOR'S NOTES

The first time I went to Cancun and saw the white sandy beaches and turquoise water, I was hooked. That was in the 90's, and I immediately purchased a two-bedroom villa timeshare and managed to vacation in Mexico for the next 20-plus years.

The Royal Resorts were built by four Ex-military Americans back in the 70's, and a couple of the owners built their own homes a little way down the beach from The Royal Mayan. After walking by one of the houses each year on our daily beach walking excursions, I decided there had to be a romance story somewhere in the resort's history. I used a lot of actual places in the Cancun area in the story, although some are no longer there. The Royal Mayan, The Royal Caribbean, and The Royal Islander are all gone now, too, but the families who vacationed at them for over 30 years will remember their happy memories forever.

I hope James and Annika's story will allow The Royal Resorts properties—The Royal Mayan, The Royal Caribbean and The Royal Islander—located next to each other on a prime Cancun beach location for over a quarter of a century to live on for years to come in my romance story, *Lost in Cancun.*

Cancun is my favorite winter vacation spot, where I still enjoy vacationing every year. Their other resorts —The Royal Cancun, The Royal Sands, The Royal Haciendas, and The Grand Residences — are still around. If you get the chance to experience one or all of them, I hope you'll love it as much as I do!

RECIPE

MEXICAN STREET TACOS

INGREDIENTS

- 2 tablespoons reduced sodium soy sauce
- 2 tablespoons freshly squeezed lime juice
- 2 tablespoons canola oil, *divided*
- 3 cloves garlic, *minced*
- 2 teaspoons chili powder
- 1 teaspoon ground cumin
- 1 teaspoon dried oregano
- 1 1/2 pounds skirt steak, *cut into 1/2-inch pieces*
- 12 mini flour tortillas, *warmed*
- 3/4 cup diced red onion
- 1/2 cup chopped fresh cilantro leaves
- 1 lime, *cut into wedges*

INSTRUCTIONS

- In a medium bowl, combine soy sauce, lime juice, 1

tablespoon canola oil, garlic, chili powder, cumin and oregano.

- In a gallon-size Ziploc bag or large bowl, combine the soy sauce mixture and steak; marinate for at least 1 hour up to 4 hours, turning the bag occasionally.
- Heat the remaining 1 tablespoon canola oil in a large skillet over medium-high heat. Add steak and marinade, and cook, stirring often, until the steak has browned and the marinade has reduced, about 5-6 minutes, or until desired doneness.
- Serve steak in tortillas, topped with onion, cilantro and lime.

yield: 6 servings
cook: 15 minutes
total: 1 hour 30 minutes

RECIPE

CHOCOLATE BUTTERMILK CAKE WITH FROSTING

Ingredients
    1 cup butter

    1/3 cup unsweetened cocoa

    1 cup water

    1/2 cup buttermilk

    2 large eggs

    1 teaspoon baking soda

    1 teaspoon vanilla

    2 cups sugar

    2 cups all-purpose flour

    1/4 teaspoon salt

Chocolate-Buttermilk Frosting
    1 cup butter

    1/4 cup unsweetened cocoa

    1/3 cup buttermilk

    2 cups confectioners' sugar

    1 teaspoon vanilla

    1/2 cup toasted pecans (optional)

Instructions

Preheat oven to 350 degrees and grease a 9X13-inch pan.

In a small bowl, melt butter in the microwave. Add cocoa and hot water, stirring until smooth.

Using an electric mixer, beat buttermilk, eggs, baking soda, and vanilla until smooth in a large bowl. Gradually add the melted butter mixture.

Add sugar, flour and salt to the buttermilk mixture and beat until blended.

Pour batter into prepared pan. Bake for 30 to 35 minutes, or until set in the middle.

To make frosting, combine melted butter, cocoa, and buttermilk in a medium bowl. Stir constantly, until the mixture is smooth. Add in confectioners' sugar, vanilla, and pecans.

Pour over the cake while the cake is still warm. Let frosting cool and set before slicing.

ROSE MARIE MEUWISSEN

Rose Marie Meuwissen, a first-generation Norwegian American born and raised in Minnesota, always tries to incorporate her Norwegian heritage into her writing. After receiving a BA in Marketing from Concordia University, a Master's in Creative Writing from Hamline University soon followed. Minnesota is still where she calls home.

She has traveled around the world, including Scandinavia, but still has many places to see, enjoys attending Scandinavian events, writing conferences and is usually busy writing Minnesota Lakes Contemporary Romances, Viking Time Travel Romances or Norwegian Traditions Children's Books.

Visit her at www.rosemariemeuwissen.com

ALSO BY ROSE MARIE MEUWISSEN

NOVELS

- ***Taking Chances***—a contemporary romance novel set in Minnesota and Arizona.
- ***Married by Saturday***—a contemporary romance novel set in Minnesota and Montana.
- ***Accidental Vegas Bride***—a contemporary romance novel set in Minnesota and Vegas.
- ***Looking for Mr. Right***—a contemporary internet dating romance novel set on Prior Lake in Minnesota.
- ***Lost in Cancun***—a 1994 second-chances romance novel set in Minnesota and Cancun, Mexico. Book One in The Royal Resorts Series.

NOVELLAS

- ***Annika—A Christmas Romance***—a contemporary romance set in Minnesota with a Nordic theme during the Christmas Holidays.
- ***Skol! Viking Blonde Ale***—a Nordic contemporary romance set in Minnesota at an Autumn festival complete with a fortune teller, Nordic ale and Vikings!
- ***Choosing to Live***—a Norwegian woman's journey during WWII to survive the Nazi Occupation of Norway—***Coming soon!***

CHILDREN'S BOOKS

REAL NORWEGIANS SERIES

- ***Real Norwegians Eat Lutefisk***—a Children's book about the tradition of Lutefisk presented in both English and Norwegian.
- ***Real Norwegians Eat Rømmegrøt***—the second Children's book in the series about the tradition of Rømmegrøt presented in both English and Norwegian.
- ***Real Norwegians Eat Lefse***—the third Children's book in the series about the tradition of Lefse presented in both English and Norwegian.
- ***Real Norwegians Eat Krumkake***—the fourth Children's book in the series about the tradition of Krumkake presented in both English and Norwegian **—Coming next!**

NOVELETTES

MINNESOTA LAKES ROMANCES

- ***Hot Summer Nights***—a Summer romance set in Prior Lake, Minnesota on Prior Lake.
- ***Railroad Ties***—an Autumn romance set in Two Harbors, Minnesota on Lake Superior.
- ***Blizzard of Love***—a Winter romance set in Lutsen, Minnesota on Lake Superior.
- ***Nor-Way to Love***—a Spring romance set in Minneapolis, Minnesota on Lake Harriet.
- ***Old Yule Log Fires***—a Christmas romance set in Excelsior, Minnesota on Lake Minnetonka.
- ***A Kiss Under the Northern Lights***—a Summer romance set in Ely, Minnesota on Big Lake.
- ***Dancing in the Moonlight***—a Summer romance set on Mille Lacs Lake, Minnesota.
- ***Dance of Love***—a Festival romance set at the Renaissance Fair in Shakopee, Minnesota.
- ***A Date for Valentine's Day***—a Holiday romance set at Lafayette Country Club on Lake Minnetonka, Minnesota.

- ***Lakes, Loons & Lutefisk***—a Summer Festival Nordic romance set at the Looney Days event on Loon Lake in Vergas, Minnesota.

POETRY COLLECTION

COMING SOON!

- ***Christmas Notes***—a collection of Christmas prose poems to warm the heart during the Christmas season.

ALSO BY ROSE MARIE MEUWISSEN

LOOKING FOR MR. RIGHT

by

Rose Marie Meuwissen

LOOKING FOR MR. RIGHT— COPYRIGHT

Print ISBN: 978-1-954030-04-6

Published in the United States of America

Nordic Publishing

Edited by Leanore Elliot and Rose Marie Meuwissen

Cover Design by Rose Marie Meuwissen

Rocki

Internet dating wasn't something Rocki Sandstrom ever thought she would try. When her best friend insisted, they set up online profiles to search for Mr. Right. Only because she was positive it wouldn't work. But when Rocki literally met Mr. Wrong who suggested there was nothing wrong with having a little fun while she kept looking for Mr. Right, she actually saw some truth in the idea. What could it hurt?

Will Rocki find her Mr. Right? Or will she only find Mr. Wrong?

Dominick

Dominick Taggart believed internet dating couldn't possibly help anyone find their person. He felt so strongly about it that he decided to write his Master's Thesis on it. The only way to get first-hand knowledge on the subject was to sign up for Life Match Dating. His theory was that women looked for Mr. Right but wanted Mr. Wrong. Why couldn't he be both?

Will Dominick be proved wrong and actually find his person?

LOOKING FOR MR. RIGHT
—CHAPTER ONE

"I deserve a man who wants only me!" Rocki Sandstrom faced the mirror to check out the reflection of the woman staring back at her. Hell, she looked damn good, still! After all, she was only a little over forty. Dang, but she felt old these days, even though she still looked hot. At least, she thought so. What was wrong with her that she couldn't find a man? Well, it definitely wasn't because she hadn't found any, because she had. Unfortunately for both her and them, she just didn't like any of them. Enough, that was. Actually, it wasn't that they weren't likeable, they simply didn't make her blood run hot. Not even warm. She wanted blood to rush through her entire body in a heated response to a man's touch.

"Rocki? You ready to go?" Allisa asked, as she walked in through the front door of Rocki's lavish two-story executive house in Prior Lake.

"Coming!" Rocki yelled down, above the railing overlooking the front foyer. "I'll be down in a minute."

"You look great. In fact, you look hot!" Allisa walked into the great room adjoining the kitchen and took a seat on a stool at the breakfast bar.

Rocki picked out a matching black leather purse with lots of gold bling to go with her outfit of black skin tight jeans tucked into three-inch heeled black leather boots, also boasting gold bling. Then grabbed a black leather jacket to go over her low-cut, blousy, gold knit top cinched at the waist by a wide black leather belt. Finally, she made it down the staircase to the Great Room.

"It's about time," Allisa said smiling. "Sure you're ready now?"

"Do you think I look okay?"

"Of course, you do, but that's not the question you should ask. The real question is will any of the guys look good enough to suit your tastes?"

"Are you insinuating I'm fussy?" Rocki asked, displaying her most sincere look.

"Oh my God! Seriously? You're so discriminatingly finicky, I really question if you'll ever find anyone who meets your standards. But let's go. I'm willing to give it a shot tonight."

"You are so reassuring, Allisa. Sometimes, I wonder why we even bother looking." Rocki set the house alarm and they finally headed out to Allisa's brand-new Camaro.

"We bother, because if we just sit here in your house all night, no Knight in Shining Armor is going to drive up into your driveway, walk up to your door and ring the doorbell. And then ask you to marry him. That's why."

"Really? What do you think the odds of that happening are?"

"Oh about, one in a million, probably."

"And what, pray tell, do you think the odds are we will find Mr. Right at the fabulous Redstone's bar tonight?" Rocki asked over the roof of the car as she got in.

Allisa started the engine. "More than one in a million because some men will be at Redstone's. And there are no men at your house, so the odds will at least be in our favor at the bar. Besides, where else can we meet eligible men?" She scrolled down her cell phone's music playlist to one of their signature songs-*I Will Survive*-and cranked up the volume on the stereo.

They both sang along to the words as she backed out of the driveway.

Twenty minutes later, they arrived at Redstone's and valet parked the car. Allisa and Rocki could feel the vibrations of the music before they even walked through the entrance doors. Music was their thing. It calmed them and made them forget about everything else except the way the rhythm made them want to move their bodies in sensual unison with each beat.

They found seats at the bar and ordered glasses of Beringer's White Zinfandel wine. Each scanned the crowd to look over the prospects for the evening. It wasn't uncommon for neither one of them to find even one man who looked interesting to them. It seemed tonight wouldn't be any different, but the night was still young and there was no telling who may walk through the doors as the evening progressed. There was always a chance, slight though it may be and they each only needed one good man.

The question they kept asking themselves was where could they find one?

Rocki dejectedly looked at the sorry loser men surrounding them and felt like her goal was becoming more hopeless as each year passed by. She'd been divorced for three years now. Her ex had been restless for the last few years of their marriage. She'd known that, yes, but she thought he would get over his misguided notion that he was missing out on something. He ultimately came to the conclusion he couldn't find it while staying married to her. So, the week after their daughter left for college, he packed his stuff and left.

Rocki thought her life had surely ended that day, but she still had two children who loved her and brought happiness to her life. She liked being married, having someone to come home to and someone to do things with. Their sex life had always been good. Filled with passion. She really missed the sex. He was probably out having sex right now, with whomever he wanted to, which totally pissed her off. She, on the other hand, hadn't had sex since he'd left. Her friends told her to buy sex toys to relieve the sexual tension, but she wanted a live warm body to hold onto while she was having an orgasm, so she hadn't taken them up on their suggestions.

A couple, just about her and Allisa's age, sat down on stools next to Rocki.

She couldn't help but overhear bits and pieces of their conversation. One statement totally caught her attention. They had met on an internet dating service. Wow!

The couple got up to make their way to the dance floor.

"Allisa, I just overheard them saying they met on an internet dating service."

"Really. I heard some women at work talking about internet dating. Some have had bad luck and some have met good people," Allisa stated.

"It seems scary. How do you know if they are predators or stalkers or who knows?" Rocki asked.

"How do you know these guys here aren't predators or stalkers? You don't."

"I guess you're right. Should we just go home right now and maybe hibernate for the rest of our lives? Not take any chances because we might get hurt?" Rocki stared hopelessly at the dance floor.

"Whatever!" Allisa rolled her eyes. "From what I heard about internet dating, it does all the work for you as far as matching your likes and dislikes, religious beliefs, political views, etc. You can even look for an educated man with a great career and income. You certainly can't do that here by just looking at them. I think it would be a lot easier than this."

"Are you saying you want to try it?"

Allisa shrugged. "I don't know. It's scary, but so is this and we don't seem to be getting anywhere this way."

"You've got a point there." Rocki watched a man approach them.

"Would you beautiful ladies like to dance with me and my friend?" the man asked.

Rocki looked him over and really didn't see anything she liked, but answered, "And where's your friend?"

"I'll get him and be right back," he said and left.

A couple of minutes later, he walked back up with an older, grungy-looking bald man who reeked of cigarettes and alcohol.

He stood seemingly waiting for a response from her. "So do you ladies want to dance with me and my friend?" he asked again.

Rocki stared him directly in the eye and gave him her response, "I don't think so. Actually, there isn't a chance in Hell, we will be dancing with you or your friend."

He stared at her in disbelief, as if she hadn't actually just said what she'd said to him.

Rocki didn't flinch but instead held her stare.

He nodded, turned, motioned to his friend and left.

Allisa stared at Rocki in her own disbelief at what she'd just heard. "Oh, my God! I can't believe you just said that to them!"

"Were you going to dance with his friend?" Rocki asked straight-faced.

"Hell, no!"

"Okay then. Neither was I. I figured if he had the gall to think either of us would, he got no more than he deserved."

Both Rocki and Allisa broke out in uncontrollable laughter and had to hold on to the bar counter, so they wouldn't fall off their bar stools.

Needless to say, no one else approached them the rest of the night and they were perfectly all right with that. They talked, laughed, and danced to their favorite songs with each other until the band quit playing for the evening. Who knows? Maybe the men at Redstone's thought they were a couple, but they didn't care because there wasn't even one man in the whole bar that interested either of them.

They'd had enough fun by midnight for one evening, so they

headed outside to pick up the Camaro at the valet stand. The convertible top was down in minutes, and their long hair was quickly put into ponytails. Allisa scrolled down her cell phone playlist to the most appropriate song for their ride home, *Holding out for a Hero*, and cranked up the volume. They sang along to the song as loud as they could.